BREAK ME

GENEVA LEE

ALSO BY GENEVA LEE

THE RIVALS SAGA
Blacklist
Backlash
Bombshell

THE ROYALS SAGA
Command Me
Conquer Me
Crown Me
Crave Me
Covet Me
Capture Me
Complete Me
Cross Me
Claim Me
Consume Me
Breathe Me
Break Me

THE SINNERS SAGA
Beautiful Criminal
Beautiful Sinner
Beautiful Forever

The Sins That Bind Us

THE ROYALS SAGA: TWELVE

BREAK ME

GENEVA LEE

IVY ESTATE
SEATTLE

BREAK ME

Copyright © 2020 by Geneva Lee.

All rights reserved.

This book or any portion thereof may not be reproduced or used in any manner whatsoever without the express written permission of the publisher except for the use of brief quotations in a book review.

This is a work of fiction. Names, characters, businesses, places, events and incidents are either the products of the author's imagination or used in a fictitious manner. Any resemblance to actual persons, living or dead, or actual events is purely coincidental.

Ivy Estate Publishing + Media

www.GenevaLee.com

First published, 2020.

Cover design © Date Book Designs.

Image © Andrey Kiselev/Adobe Stock.

To Josh,
Every love story is about you

1

BELLE

The cold is so deep it sinks into my skin and settles in my bones. The wind slices through the air around me, catching my hair and whipping it across my face. All I can see is white. There's no sound except the faint cry of the wind that sends snowflakes dancing around me. It's oddly peaceful despite the chill. A wail rises up, shattering the still morning. It's distant. Foreign. *A baby?*

I want to turn to the sound, to find the child and comfort it, but it's too far away from me. Soon the pressing roar of silence overwhelms the noise once more, until there is only me caught in my wintery snow globe. Pins prick my fingertips, my skin growing too cold in the dropping temperature, but I don't mind. I haven't felt this relaxed in ages. Why can't it always be like this?

Calm.

Peaceful.

Alone.

A small voice taps at the back of my mind, whispering

thoughts I don't want to interrupt me. *She's better off without you*, it murmurs, *but what kind of mother would you be if you left her? Take her with you. She's already here. It will be easy and then she'll stop crying. You'll both stop crying. Things will finally be better.*

I take a step forward, moving closer to that blank oblivion in front of me that promises to set me free.

The voice is always with me now. It comes to me in my sleep and whispers the truth I try to ignore during the day. It's right. We'll both be happier once we find shelter in the peaceful cold waiting to embrace us. I can't leave Penny behind. I'm responsible for her. And somewhere deep inside me, I know that I love her. Maybe I can find that feeling on the other side of this—in that place where we're safe and happy again.

"Belle!"

It's not the tiny voice calling my name. She never says my name. This voice is deep, radiating with authority, although a tinge of panic ripples under its command. Part of me wants to turn to it and explain that everything is fine. I finally figured it out. I just have to go towards the cold, bright light, and then Penny and I will be free. I can finally be the mother she needs. I won't be scared or helpless. We just have to find that promised place, the one the voice whispers will deliver me.

"Beautiful!" The other voice cried again, and the world latched onto me. A new thought formed in my head: Smith. He could come with us.

No, the voice whispers. *He won't understand.*

For the first time, doubt rose inside me. The voice

didn't know Smith like I did. He'd understand. He'd want to go.

No! I told you—you can't tell him about me, the voice says.

I ignored her, turning slowly, still safe in the wintry peace whirling around me. My eyes met his, locking on, but before I could call him to join me, he pleaded, "Beautiful, come to me."

I blinked, and suddenly Smith seemed so far away. His arms reached out to me, his words begging me to move towards him. It took a moment for me to understand. Why would he want me to leave this peaceful place? But his words drew me to him, and the world slowly returned to me. A baby cried again, and I remembered that Penny was in my arms. I glanced down to comfort her and spotted the ice below me.

"Smith? Where...?" But I didn't need him to tell me.

I didn't know how I got there. I didn't know where I was going. Suddenly, the slight prickles of cold I'd felt ached to life across my body. I clutched Penny more tightly against me, worried that my increasingly numb hands might drop her. I was too scared to move, frozen not only by the cold but also the terror pulsing through me. Why was I here? What had happened? I waited for the little voice to tell me, but she'd gone silent.

Smith came as close to the edge of the ice as he dared, urging me forward with a firm voice that rattled with an undercurrent of fear I felt myself. I forced myself toward him, slipping one foot forward across the thinly frozen surface of the pond. I could see water rippling beneath it.

Then a small line etched across it and splintered near my feet. My heart nearly stopped. Smith was in front of me, I reminded myself. Penny was in my arms. The ice was cracking along with my own mind. It took every ounce of effort to propel myself forward. As soon as I was close enough, Smith's arm lashed out and caught me around the waist. He pulled me against him as the ice on the pond gave way. I'd been standing there only seconds ago. If he hadn't come — if he hadn't found me... I couldn't bring myself to think what would have happened.

We crushed Penny between us as I held onto him, his own arms tightened around me. "Smith...Smith. Help me. I don't know why..."

I didn't understand any of this. I didn't understand myself.

Smith said nothing for a long moment. He only stared into my eyes before he pressed a palm to cup the nape of my neck and pull me closer to him. Neither of us spoke. Finally, he drew back and searched my face. He was looking for answers.

I hoped he would find some there, so that he could share them.

"It's okay," he said, sounding as if the words were meant as much for him as for me. "You're safe. Everything's fine."

I shook my head, moving away from him. I held Penny against his chest until his hands moved from me to cradle her. I didn't want to hold her. I didn't want to hurt her.

"It's not okay," I choked. I couldn't explain any of this. Not to him. Not to me. "Smith, I think I'm going crazy."

2

SMITH

Penny laid on the changing table wrapped in a blanket while I counted her fingers and toes. I kissed and rubbed each of her chilled limbs, drawing away the bluish tinge until she was a warm, rosy pink again. Movement caught my eye and I looked up to see Nora edging nervously into the room with a freshly warmed bottle. My heart sank when I realized it was her. Belle refused to go inside the nursery. Part of me was grateful. The truth was that no matter how much I focused on the crisis at hand, I couldn't get the image of her on the ice, holding our daughter, out of my mind. I suspected that some day when my eyes closed the final time, it would be the last thing I saw. A memory like that carved itself into your bones and became part of you. The other part of me wondered how this would change my wife, and how long Belle would punish herself for her strange behavior.

"She's hungry," I said, lifting her into my arms and carrying her to the glider. A freshly lit fire crackled in the nursery hearth, and I cradled Penny close as Nora brought me the bottle. She lingered in the nursery, showing me exactly how to give Penny a bottle, but not saying much else.

"She's fine," Nora said softly after a few minutes of awkward silence.

"I know," I snapped. "Belle would never hurt her."

Nora took a startled step away, her hand fluttering to her chest as she shook her head. Her own dark eyes welling with tears. "I didn't mean to imply —"

"I'm sorry," I said, coming to my senses when I saw her horror-stricken face. Was I the monster behind all this fear? "I'm just on edge."

"I understand." But she maintained her distance and started busying herself with various chores in the nursery.

It was her job to look after the baby. She was back now, which meant there would be a second set of eyes on Penny. That should make me feel more reassured, but I wasn't positive that it would be enough. I found myself wanting to build a fortress around my daughter and my wife. The question was should I put them in separate towers or keep them together?

In my darkest thoughts, I considered whether Penny might not be safe with Belle. I hated to even admit that to myself. But Belle had taken her on the ice. And the look she gave me when she turned to me—it was like peering into the eyes of a stranger. It wasn't my wife holding our child. I didn't understand what was happening to Belle, but I would do everything in my power to find out. Until then, I had to decide whether I could trust her with the baby.

Belle would never forgive herself if something happened to Penny. I knew that. I also knew she worried that she didn't love her baby enough. I wished she could see what I did. I saw her love every time they were together. I knew it was love that drove Belle to hand the baby to someone else as she became more scared of herself. Sometimes love meant letting go. But I didn't want to let go of Belle, and I didn't want her to let go of me or Penny. I had to find her. I had to help her. And the first step to doing that was to stop avoiding each other. We had to get through this together.

I rose slowly. Penny squawked at being disturbed, closing one hand over the bottle and the other around my finger. I stared down at her to find her blue eyes watching me and knew I had to put her above everyone, even Belle. It was what Belle would want me to do. I had to keep Penny safe until Belle was herself again, and she would be—soon. I couldn't consider anything else.

"Would you like me to take her?" Nora asked carefully, obviously still shaken by my outburst. She hovered near a stack of freshly folded receiving blankets.

I nodded. "Please. I should check on my wife."

"I saw her," Nora murmured as I moved closer. "She's not herself. She's no more to blame than you are."

"I know." I passed Penny to her, earning me a mewl of disapproval until Nora snuggled her to her chest.

Thankfully, Nora's attention shifted instantly to her charge. I couldn't handle a lecture from my nanny about how to be a husband and father. I was perfectly proficient at fucking that up without her insight.

"Pretty baby," she cooed. "You need a nap." She carried her back to the chair by the fire, lowered herself, and began to rock.

I lingered in the doorway and watched her. She made it look easy. It was what I had imagined it to be like for Belle. I'd expected to come home from the office to find her peacefully rocking her daughter just like this. Instead, she wouldn't go near her.

Stepping into the hallway, I gathered myself for a moment, running a hand along the back of my neck while trying to figure out what to do next. Before I could, Mrs. Winters bustled by with a tea tray.

She paused to deliver a stern look. "You should see your wife now."

"I'm on my way," I said wearily. She needed to be reminded of who was in charge here, but I didn't have it in me to insult the entire staff today. Not now that I needed them more than ever.

Edward met us at the door, flashing me a concerned look as he lowered his voice, "She won't say anything," he told me. "I'll be right down the hall if you need me to help with anything."

He clapped a hand on my shoulder as he passed. He'd been nearly as shaken as I was when we got Belle off the ice. Everything had happened so quickly that I was still processing the events that led us there. The morning had started in panic when Belle couldn't seem to nurse Penny. I'd gone off to the shops to pick up formula, and I'd found out there had been a mistake with the tea she'd been drinking. Instead of helping her build her milk supply to get the baby's weight up, it had been slowly drying it out. I thought that was going to be the worst news of the day—until I reached home and found the front door wide open, Belle gone along with our daughter. I'd left Edward with her and the baby, and it was clear from his downcast eyes that he felt responsible for her winding up out there.

It wasn't his fault, though. I should have never left. I should've sent him into town, or Mrs. Winters, or waited for Nora to show up. I should have known better than to let Belle out of my sight. No one could be trusted to care as much about her safety as I did. Even her best friend.

Belle ignored Mrs. Winters as she set the tea tray on the nightstand by her side of the bed. A large cashmere blanket was wrapped around my wife's petite shoulders. She clutched it to her chest, staring at the wall without blinking.

"Let's see to getting you warmed up," Mrs. Winters said in a cheerful, but strained voice. "You'll feel fine again in no time."

Belle's eyes flashed up to her, a sneer curling her lip, morphing her face into something so cruel that I stepped forward in shock. "Fine? Don't you mean mental?"

Mrs. Winters startled for a moment, but collected herself quickly. "We all have strange fits every now and then."

"Would you excuse us a moment, Mrs. Winters?" I asked her.

She tossed a withering look at me as she made her way into the bathroom, calling over her shoulder, "I'm going to run you a hot bath."

That was a good idea. I should have thought of it. Clearly, the cook thought so as well. "Thank you." I got the oddest sense that I'd hurt her feelings by asking her to leave, but it wasn't as though she could make this matter any better. The only way we were going to help the situation was by facing it as a couple.

"I don't want a bath," Belle muttered, her words nearly lost as the sound of running water filled the air.

"It's a good idea, beautiful. It was cold out there," I said. "I think it would be a good idea if you had a little help when you are taking care of Penny."

"That's what Nora is supposed to be for," she said coldly. Each word felt like a brick being laid between us. She was building a wall around herself. I didn't need to build her a fortress. She was doing it on her own.

"Nora can't be here all the time," I said in a measured tone. "I know Edward is here, but maybe we should call your aunt."

"You really don't trust me," she said in a small voice, plunging forward before I could assuage her fears. "Good. You shouldn't trust me. I don't trust me."

"Whatever's happening, I swear to you that we will figure it out."

"I know." But there was no confidence in her eyes, all I found there was defeat.

3

BELLE

I hated the patterned paper covering the walls. I'd been staring at it for the better part of half an hour while Mrs. Winters and Smith clucked over me. Penny had been taken to the nursery for a bottle. It was the first time I hadn't been the one to feed her. Instead, I sat here staring at the fucking walls. I'd picked out the floral wallpaper, thinking its lush green colors would provide a sensual backdrop to our bedroom. I must not have looked closely enough, because I hadn't seen what was hidden in the print until it had been applied to every wall in the bedroom. Small spiders had been painted on to the rose petals, nearly blending into the lush background. I'd only noticed them recently. Now I couldn't see anything else. Sometimes, I was convinced they were crawling across the leaves.

"Beautiful, what are you looking at?"

I tore my gaze away and shook my head as he studied the spot I'd been staring at. Could he see the spiders? "My mind must have wandered."

Poor choice of words. Was that what had happened earlier on the ice? Suddenly, I couldn't stop thinking of moments I couldn't explain. Putting the photograph of Margot in Smith's desk drawer. Forgetting the nappies on the changing table. I hadn't even checked the tea I had been given by the pharmacist. It was a wonder that something worse hadn't happened.

Well, it almost had.

A shiver rolled up my back, turning into a full tremble that overtook my body until I was shaking like the leaves the spiders crawled across on the wallpaper. Smith reached for my hand, pulling me up from the bed so that he could wrap his strong arms around me. But the instinct I usually had—the one that sent me melting against my husband's chest—was gone. I stood, locked in the spot, letting him hold me, but wanting something much darker than comfort.

"You should drink your tea," Mrs. Winters announced, ignoring our embrace and bustling around us to pour me a cup. Before she could hand it to me, Smith intercepted it and raised it to his nose.

"This is the new one?" he asked.

"Lord knows. It was in the bag from the shops." She looked at him as though he'd lost his mind.

I couldn't help wondering what she thought of us. The frantic, incompetent young mother and her suspicious, mysterious husband. But whatever she thought of us, Smith seemed reassured by her answer.

"You should drink this," he coaxed.

I arched an eyebrow, trying to get a read on what was going on with him. At least if I was going mental, I wouldn't be alone. "Has it been approved by my poison tester?"

"There's something I need to tell you," he said, sounding uncharacteristically nervous. Given that he'd been moments from watching his wife and child die, I couldn't exactly blame him. "Why don't you sit back down?"

I did as he suggested, more than willing to follow his orders. If I listened to him, he would keep me safe. That's what I needed him to do. Smith would make the decisions. Or Edward. Or whoever was around and still had a functioning brain in their skull. I wrapped my hands around the teacup, letting its warmth seep into my skin, but my trembling continued. The day had been cold, but my physical reaction had less to do with the weather and more to do with my close call.

"It's about the tea," he said, and I looked at him in surprise. "You got the wrong one. There must have been a mixup at the pharmacy. The tea you were drinking decreases milk supply."

"What?" I blinked at him. That didn't make sense. "I read the box."

"It didn't come in that tin?" he asked.

"I put it in the tin to keep it fresh," Mrs. Winters interjected. She twisted her fingers together, looking back and forth between the two of us as she confessed. "I should have asked."

"Why?" I asked slowly.

"When you brought it home from the doctor, I assumed you wanted your supply to dry up," Mrs. Winters admitted.

"Why would I want that?" A strange urge to cry took hold of me.

"I'm not in the business of prying," she said softly. "You went to the doctor and you came back with a prescription. I assumed you couldn't nurse the baby and needed to take it. I didn't feel it was my station to ask."

"But you knew what it would do?" I asked, shocked.

"I thought you knew. When I found the box sitting in the kitchen and you told me you needed to take it..." She trailed away. Gathering her courage, she lifted her shoulders and looked squarely at me. "I'm very sorry that this happened."

"An honest mistake then," Smith said, his face unreadable. I knew my husband well enough to see that part of him wanted to strangle her for the mistake—the part of him that wanted to protect me at all costs.

I took a sip of the tea, wrinkling my nose with displeasure at its taste.

"The pharmacist said it tastes like licorice," Smith told me.

"It does." I abandoned the cup back on the tray and sighed. "There's no point to it, I've already dried up."

"The pharmacist said..."

But I wasn't listening to him. I was tired of pretending I could solve these problems with medication or herbs or hired help. Whatever was happening to me, it was beyond the scope of traditional care. I would do everything Smith suggested, but I wouldn't delude myself as to what the results would be.

And I never allow my baby to suffer like that again. I

could still hear her screams, the sound of them was branded on my soul. I had done that to her through my own negligence and through pride. I had no business keeping formula out of the house. How did I not foresee what would happen if I couldn't nurse her?

Smith's lecture on restarting my milk supply was interrupted by a knock on the door. He turned and called out a welcome.

Nora's head appeared through a crack in the door. "She's asleep. Poor angel was exhausted. She took the whole bottle, though."

"Thank you," Smith said shortly. He'd never liked her. I could sense it. I just didn't understand why. I found myself wishing he liked her more. She would make a better mother than me.

"Please keep an eye on her?" Smith asked Nora. "Belle is going to take a bath."

"Of course," she said brightly, disappearing from view. Maybe her way of coping with trauma was to put on a happy face and add a spoonful of sugar. I couldn't help but wonder where she found this unlimited supply of sunshine from, though. I was glad she was here to take care of Penny, since I continued to prove myself completely useless. But I didn't think I could stomach her bright smile a minute longer.

It wasn't that I didn't like Nora. She was helpful to have around. But she was also a constant reminder that I'd utterly failed my own child.

"Your bath is ready, ma'am," Mrs. Winters announced.

She bowed slightly and headed toward the door. "I'll be downstairs if you need me."

I didn't resist as he led me to the bathroom. This was how it needed to be. Smith would direct my days and I would finally get better or I wouldn't, but, at least, I wouldn't put myself or anyone else in danger. He'd never allow it.

But as he undressed me, he kept his eyes trained away from me. His hands didn't linger on my skin. When he helped me into the warm water, he turned to leave. I grabbed his hand.

"Don't leave me," I blurted out.

His throat slid as he pressed his lips into a flat line. He pulled the stool from my vanity, its metal feet scraping shrilly against the tile floor, and sat next to me. I tucked my legs against my chest and held them there. The chill I'd felt in my skin slowly disappeared, but the one that clung to my bones lingered.

Smith couldn't even look at me. I couldn't blame him for that. I tried to imagine what he must think of me now. A tear leaked from my eye and ran down my cheek. If he noticed, he didn't seem to care. He didn't move from the spot until I pulled the plug. He stood with a towel as the water began to circle the drain. Smith wrapped it around me before he helped me out of the tub.

He followed me into the bedroom, disappeared inside the closet, and came out holding a robe.

I shook my head, tears beginning to fall more freely now. "Smith," I croaked. "I need you."

I was in his arms instantly. He gazed down on me with

a look of total adoration. I fought the urge to turn away. I didn't deserve that look. Not after what I had done. Not after what I put him through.

"I need you," I repeated, pressing my palms to his chest as if to prove to myself that he was really here with me. I no longer felt certain of anything.

"Beautiful," he coaxed, "I'm right here. I'll protect you."

"I don't want you to protect me," I said, casting my eyes to the floor. I became increasingly interested in my toes. I wasn't entirely sure where the embarrassment came from. Smith and I had never suffered from nerves where intimacy was concerned, but I wasn't asking him for sex. Not this time.

"What are you saying?" he asked slowly.

"I need you to help me escape," I said, quickly adding, "I mean, subspace. I can't stand feeling like this. Take it away."

Smith hesitated, his eyes raking across me as a worried frown tugged on his lips. "I'm not sure —"

"I am," I cut him off. It was the first thing I had felt certain of for a very long time. My surety ran bone deep. Smith was the only one who could release me from this, and I needed him in a way I had never needed him before.

I'd always wanted him. I craved submitting to his dominance. It wasn't something I understood exactly, but something that just made sense from the first time he touched me. This was different. I needed something else entirely. Yes, I needed to give him total control. I needed to feel safe. I needed to know that my own fate wasn't in my hands but his, because I trusted him more than I trusted myself. Those were all things he could do without touching me.

Now? I needed him to punish me.

"I'll give you whatever you need," he promised. "But you have nothing to run from. Whatever's going on, will figure it out together."

I nodded, mostly to placate him, though. The truth was that we weren't going to figure this out. We'd been trying to do just that. Something was wrong with me. I couldn't shake the sense that I was unraveling from within. And I needed a way to live with this fact. He could help me escape the darkness clouding my mind, but only by stripping away the anger I felt with myself. There was only one way I could think of.

I dropped the towel.

"Now?" Smith stared at me.

I nodded furiously. I couldn't live like this for one more second, I had to have release.

"There's something I need to tell you," he started. "You're not going to be happy—"

"After." I closed the space between us and smashed my mouth to his. That was all it took. Smith responded as he always did, with a brutal masculinity that my body recognized. I whimpered into the kiss. I didn't deserve this. I didn't deserve him, but I was too selfish to deny myself. We broke apart, he stepped back and studied me. But it wasn't the predatory look he usually gave me, the one he leveled at me when he was deciding what delicious way he planned to torture me.

He inspected me like he was looking for cracks. Would he find them? Was he scared he would break me?

"Fuck me," I begged, unable to stand another moment of crushing reality. "Take me. Use me. Free me."

Punish me.

Something held me back from speaking those words aloud. My husband had tested me before at the beginning of our relationship. But punishment? That wasn't generally on the table. Smith was dominant in nature, and I knelt before him in submission, but that didn't mean that he was my master. Far from it. He took my body as he saw fit, and I gave it to him willingly. I'd seen other relationships—darker relationships—and I knew that his penchant wasn't for inflicting actual pain. At least, I had not known pain at his hands. I'd seen him, though, in some of the secret places we had visited. I'd also seen how the people there responded to his presence. I'd often suspected my husband kept parts of himself from me. He claimed that he'd been twisted and warped by Hammond, who'd acted as a surrogate father when he was young. But I'd also watched him kill a man without hesitation. He was capable of things more dark than most people ever dreamed of, and it was that wickedness I craved in him now.

A shadow crossed over his face and his eyes hardened into cold emeralds. He snapped his fingers. "On your knees."

"Yes, sir," I said in relief, dropping to them. I rocked back on my heels, hands folded in my lap as he circled to inspect me.

"Show me your breasts."

I moved my hands behind my back, gripping each wrist so that my chest was thrust forward for his pleasure. Smith bent to place his index finger under my chin and tipped my face up. I held my breath in anticipation.

"So beautiful. I think I'd like to watch you suck my cock."

My eyes flickered to his groin and the unmistakable outline of his erection straining against his jeans. I knew better than to reach for him. I looked back up to Smith and waited.

"I love it when you're patient." I heard his fingers unbuckle his belt and the whoosh of it as he tugged it free from his jeans. His eyes hooded, and he groaned as he took his cock out. My tongue darted over my lips and he smirked. "It's getting harder to control yourself, isn't it?"

He bit his lower lip and I heard the rough stroke of his hand on his shaft. I squirmed in the spot as wet heat seeped from me. Finally, he took a step closer and held himself to my lips. "Suck me, beautiful."

I plunged my mouth over him, careful to keep my eyes trained upward as I took his shaft deep into my throat. His eyes squinted at the edges as he grunted his approval. Smith's hand grabbed a fistful of hair and urged my mouth to glide faster until I was practically choking as he fucked the back of my throat.

"You're going to make me come in your fucking mouth," he gritted out. "But I'm not ready to come. I have so much to do to you, but..." A low rumble cut him off as he grabbed my head with both hands and thrust himself so far that my lips smashed against his balls. I gagged a little but as the first heat spurted down my throat I instinctively relaxed, giving my body over to him entirely.

There was only pleasing him. I didn't need to breathe. I needed to give him pleasure. I didn't need to think. I needed to accept the gifts his hands and mouth and cock would give me. There was only him, erasing the world until all that remained was the tether he offered.

Smith withdrew and shook his head. "Look at what you made me do. Now I have to find a way to make myself hard again so I can fuck you properly." He considered for a moment, studying me like a connoisseur might pause to appreciate a meal before taking the first bite. "On your feet."

I scrambled up, his words an irresistible command. I was his puppet—whatever he commanded, I would do without question, without thought.

"Against the wall." I moved closer until my breasts grazed it. My nipples tightened as they made contact with the cool plaster. Smith walked behind me, placed a hand on the middle of my back and smashed me to the wall. I gasped with pleasure as the mood darkened further. He didn't kiss me, though. Instead, his other hand spread my thighs wider.

"I think this might inspire me," he growled before plunging his hand between my legs. His fingers spread my sex roughly, massaging me open so that he could shove two fingers inside me. "You're so fucking wet. You like belonging to me. You like being played with. You're my perfect fuck doll, and you want it rough, don't you?"

"Yes, sir," I panted, my cheek mashed against the wall. I

moaned as another finger made its way inside me, and another, until he had half his hand buried there. He paused to readjust, hooking a finger to hit a tender spot that belonged to him. It sent me over the edge and I exploded against his hand, soaking it entirely as my body spasmed violently. The hand pinning me to the wall was the only reason I managed to stay upright.

When he released me, I sagged as he caught me. Smith carried me to the bed and dropped me on the mattress. With one hand he flipped me to my stomach before grabbing my hips and yanking me onto his cock.

I cried out as it speared into me. There was no long, drawing strokes. He fucked me hard with a merciless rhythm that sent all my blood rushing to the spot where we were joined. There was only him and this building need. I dug my fingers into the sheets and held on.

"Let go," he ordered, and I relaxed my fingers. Without a hold on the bed, his punishing strokes pushed me forward until I was splayed against the mattress like a rag doll.

"It's time to come now," he said harshly. "Milk my cock, beautiful."

I tightened around him and let myself go, abandoning everything I was to his control.

4

SMITH

Belle hadn't stirred when I rose from bed that evening. I'd fucked her into some sort of comatose state, and while I worried that we couldn't avoid facing this much longer, I was relieved to see her at peace. I checked on Penny in the nursery before making my way to my study. I went directly to my desk, opened the drawer, and discovered the photograph of Margot staring at me.

I sank into my chair, the last tethers of hope I'd clung to slipping from my grasp. I'd gotten rid of the photograph. Thrown it out. It was back. Only Belle knew about Margot. I'd wanted to believe her when she said it was a misunderstanding before. After finding her on the ice, I no longer knew what to believe. She'd walked onto that pond with our baby. She had put this photograph in the drawer again. Had she switched her own tea? What was happening to my wife?

Humphrey appeared in the door, bowing to me as I

quickly shut the desk drawer. "Pardon me, sir, but you have a guest."

"I'm not really up to seeing anyone today." The truth was that I was tired. My head felt like I'd injected lead between my eyeballs. I no longer knew how to carry the weight of all of this, and the last thing I needed was another problem to deal with.

"I said as much," he replied tightly, "but she's quite insistent."

I groaned, my eyes closing as I pinched the bridge of my nose. "Brunette? Gorgeous but terrifying?"

"Yes," Humphrey said. "Should I tell her to come back?"

"Oh, I wouldn't do that, Humphrey." I heaved myself back up and made my way toward the door. "I'll see to her."

"Very good, sir." He backed away to allow me to exit.

"Miss Kincaid will probably be staying a while."

"The guest rooms are full," he reminded me stiffly. "There is the guest house, but it will need a thorough cleaning."

"We'll deal with it tomorrow." We'd had more than enough on the list for today.

His bushy eyebrows met like two caterpillars bumping together, but he quickly rearranged his face into subservience. "I hate to bring this up, but I should remind you that I'm leaving in the morning to visit to holiday with my family in Wales. Would you prefer if I canceled my trip?"

I stifled a groan. Now more than ever we needed

stability at Thornham, but the only person I could count on was Mrs. Winters, the least agreeable one of the bunch. I pasted a forced smile on my face. "No, of course not. I'll speak to Mrs. Price about the guest house. Georgia can take the couch tonight."

"I will see to it."

I found Georgia leaning against the wall, staring around her.

"Forget I was coming?" she asked.

"We've had some excitement here." That was a gross understatement, but she would know soon enough.

The last time I'd seen her, she'd been dressed for her part as Clara Cambridge's personal security. Today, in a black leather jacket and skin-tight dark denim jeans, she looked more like her old self right down to her knee high black boots.

"Have you ever heard the term *nouveau riche*?" she asked as I led her up the stairs toward my office.

"It cost less than our place in Holland Park," I said evenly. "Remind me where you're spending your time these days."

"I don't actually live in a castle."

"Trust me, this place is no castle." A hellscape would be a more apt description.

"What the hell is going on here, Price?" Georgia demanded as soon as we were in my study. She begrudgingly took a chair on the other side of my desk.

Instead of joining her, I unearthed a bottle of Scotch from behind a stack of boxes. I found two tumblers from the offices I'd kept in London before marrying Belle. They were filled with dust, so I wiped them out with my shirtsleeve.

"You sure know how to treat a guest," Georgia said dryly as she watched me with a smirk.

"Getting soft on me?" I asked her. "Accustomed to your meals being delivered on silver platters at the palace?"

"A girl has to have standards." She accepted the Scotch despite her commentary. "You look like a man that needs this drink. That's never a good thing."

"You're here with information," I reminded her, taking the seat across from her and staring into my own glass of amber liquid. "You tell me if I need this drink."

"What was going on out there?" Georgia asked.

I knew better than to think I would get her to talk before I came clean myself. Georgia wasn't the type of person who needed to spill a secret. She could hold on to one forever. I might have asked her to look into Thornham's history, but that didn't mean she would do me the courtesy of sharing what she found. Especially not if she felt as though she could use it as currency. It was how she operated. It was how we operated. Transactionally.

"It's a long story," I said.

"You have a full bottle of Scotch. We have time for a long story." Georgia might be abrasive, but I'd known her longer than any one else in my life. More than that, I'd grown to trust her.

I filled her in on the last few weeks worth of events, leading slowly to what had happened this morning. Georgia said nothing as I spoke, but her eyes narrowed as I finished my story and she sat down her glass, looking unnerved. I'd never seen her so obviously rattled.

"You can see what I'm up against."

"Maybe I am getting soft," she muttered. Georgia had changed since she'd gone to work for Alexander. It had been subtle at first. Sometimes, she still clung to seeing herself as the woman she'd been four years ago. She'd have to come to grips with how much she changed on her own terms. I wasn't about to force her to confront that. Still, it wasn't like her to look so worried. "You've got to do something about this, Price."

"I have a call in to the doctor. He's going to stop by the house. Maybe there's different medication she can go on," I continued before downing the rest of my drink. "Honestly, I'm not sure where to start. Distract me. Tell me what you found in the file."

"That's just it," she said slowly like I'd asked her to put her hands where I could see them. "What I found in the file isn't going to make you feel better."

At least, I wasn't surprised to hear that. "What did you find?"

"The bones are from the seventies, which means that it likely has to do with a local missing person's case."

"There was more than one person down there,' I said gruffly. The small skull floated to mind, and I shut my eyes against the image.

"There was," she confirmed grimly. "An entire family, in fact. The Thorns. Did you look into the history of this house before you bought it?"

"I know it was vacant forever. It just sat on the market."

"But that's not true. How did you hear about this house? It was vacant for years, kept up by a preservationist trust, but it wasn't for sale," she said. "It's almost like someone wanted it to stay empty."

"That's ridiculous." I stood to pour myself another Scotch. "We were told that the final member of the Thorns had passed and the house went on the market."

"Smith," Georgia said with the delicacy of someone defusing a bomb, "the house was never on the market."

"That's odd, considering I bought it," I said in a flat voice even as my heart pounded against my chest. "Our estate agent told us about it."

"You need to reach out and find out how they knew about it," Georgia said forcefully, her expression growing even grimmer. "I can't help thinking someone wanted you in this house."

"Now you sound like him," I murmured. I didn't have to tell her who I was referring to. We both knew I was speaking of Alexander. "Do you honestly think there was some conspiracy to get me into this house?"

"It's not paranoia if they're really after you," she said with a bemused smile that didn't match her worried eyes. "Maybe someone planned for you to come here."

"Who? I'm not a royal. Hammond is dead. There's not a single one of our old associates around who will care what happens to me going forward."

"Then why did you run away from London? Because you thought if you severed ties with the royal family, you'd be left alone?" she guessed.

I stared at her for a moment. It had occurred to me that that might be what this was about. But I couldn't see a reason why any of them would want to come after me. Yes, I had helped Alexander. But for the most part, our relationship had been mercenary. I'd helped him for the sake of my own wife, so she wouldn't lose her best friend. In doing so, Alexander and I had gotten along more in the past year than before, but I hardly qualified as one of his close friends or confidants. I said as much to Georgia.

She laughed. "What lies are you telling yourself? You were there with us," she reminded me. "You actively worked against MI-18."

"And what good would it do for them to come after me? I've cut ties, as you said. I doubt they have time for revenge."

"Maybe not," Georgia said, shrugging her leather clad shoulders. "But it can't be a coincidence that you wound up buying this house. Not with what's happening now. Smith, you should sit down."

It wasn't like Georgia to be so dramatic, so I did as she asked. Leaning back in my leather seat, I cupped my Scotch like a security blanket. "What happened to the family that lived here before?"

"No one knew until they found those bones," she said quietly. "They think it's them. They're the right age. They're trying to secure some type of DNA match now."

"The whole family?" I asked, recalling the pile of mixed skeletons we had discovered in the cellar. The memory of musty earth filled my mouth and nostrils. I took a drink to wash it away. "How on earth did they wind up buried in my basement?"

"Almost the whole family." Georgia hesitated.

"Just tell me," I spit out. I couldn't stand more mysteries or secrets. We had come here to start over, and somehow managed to find ourselves in the midst of another mystery.

"There were reports over the years," she began. "People swore they saw Miranda Thorne near the village or in the city."

"Miranda Thorne?"

Georgia took a deep breath. "The mother."

"People always think they're seeing ghosts," I said swiftly.

"That's just it. Smith, there were no bones that matched her age or her description." Georgia glared at me as if daring me to interrupt her again. "And then there's the stories."

We'd heard a few whisperings about Thornham since our arrival, but I'd ignored it. Now I wished I hadn't. "Village superstitions."

"Maybe," she agreed. "I would have said the same thing until you told me about Belle. The stories were that the mother went crazy. She kept claiming to hear voices. She would disappear for hours, sometimes days, and return with no explanation as to where she had been. Her husband even convinced her to see the village doctor. They were concerned she was having some type of psychotic break. She was being treated for a mental disorder."

"And?" I prompted, a pit had hollowed itself in my

stomach. I didn't want to know the answer, but I had to face it.

"And then they disappeared." Georgia swallowed a long swig of Scotch. "All of them. Vanished. The staff arrived for the day, and they were all gone. No note. No indication of where they were. The local police searched for them. They even reached out to Scotland Yard. No one ever found anything, except people who claimed to see the mother throughout the years."

"People claim to see the Loch Ness monster, too." But as much as I tried to deny the story having any relevance to my own, I couldn't. A mother slowly going crazy. A family trying to help her. That was Thornham's legacy. Was the same thing happening to Belle? I shook my head. "It's a coincidence."

"It might be," Georgia said. "But are you willing to risk your family to make a point?"

"What do you want me to do?" I looked to her, the question genuine. "Because I'm out of ideas, Georgia. I'm doing the best I can, and it's not enough. Every time I think things are getting back to normal, it gets worse."

"Maybe you should come back to London," she suggested. "Get her away from here."

"What if that's not the problem? Then I'll just be trading issues here for more issues there. I don't have an army to protect my family."

"All you have to do is ask and he'll help you," Georgia murmured.

I shook my head bitterly. The more entangled we stayed with Alexander, the worse it would be. I couldn't see any reason for MI-18 to come after me now. Maybe they weren't above revenge, but getting back in bed with the Royals would only draw more attention to us. We needed to figure out what was going on here. Whatever was happening to Belle was going on in her own mind. I refused to believe that I was living in a haunted house. Being part of a political conspiracy seemed almost as unlikely since all my enemies were dead. "I can handle things."

"I'm sure you can," Georgia said, heaving a heavy sigh that seemed to suggest she was used to having conversations with stubborn men. "Mind if I stick around anyway, though?"

It was actually a relief to have her ask. I might not agree with her theories— I suspected she'd been hanging around Alexander too long— but I trusted her. She would protect my family, and I needed the help.

"If you don't mind sharing the guesthouse," I told her. "I've asked Jane to come down and help out."

"That's a good idea." She nodded sagely. "Belle needs something to anchor her to the past."

I forced a smile and tried not to see the statement as an insult. I wanted to be the anchor tethering Belle to this life. I didn't want to have to ask for help. But I couldn't deny that I'd failed to be what she needed. I couldn't deny that she was still in danger, and I had not been able to do anything about it. I couldn't pretend I had this situation under control.

"I'm going to talk to some of the people who think they've seen Miranda over the years," Georgia told me. "And I'm going to try to find the old staff."

"Georgia, it was over forty years ago," I told her.

"Forty years for them. You're living it now," she pointed out.

As much as I wanted to argue with her, I couldn't deny that she was right.

5

BELLE

I dragged myself out of bed the next morning. I'd taken one of my sleeping pills at Smith's not-so-gentle request, and it was well past nine when I managed to gather my energy and face the day. I slipped on the velvet dressing gown Smith had given me for Christmas—sapphire blue to match my eyes, he'd said—and made my way down the spiral staircase. I'd been drinking that dreadful herbal tea for weeks. This morning I needed a proper cup of something stout and British. Passing the sitting room, movement caught my attention. I turned to stare at a mysterious pile of blankets. It stirred and I let out a little shriek. Georgia shot up, glaring, still half-asleep. Her ink-black hair was piled on top of her head in a wild bun. The blankets slipped to reveal a set of round, brown nipples. I turned away, shielding my eyes.

"Morning," she called grumpily.

"Georgia— "I said through gritted teeth as Smith came

skidding into the foyer, fully dressed in a wool sweater and jeans "—it's nice to see so much of you."

"Maybe not that much of you," Smith said dryly, casting an exasperated look her way.

Georgia stretched her arms over her head and yawned, putting even more of her ample breasts on display. "Did I forget to warn you that I sleep in the nude?"

Smith shook his head and guided me away. "Sorry about that."

"I was going for some tea to get going, but I'm awake now." I shot him a frustrated smile that was more grim than greeting.

"I think you could still use a cuppa." He navigated us towards the kitchen, taking my hand in his.

"What is she doing here?" I asked.

At least three possible excuses seemed to pass over his face judging from the way his eyes narrowed then softened, his mouth opened then closed, and his nervous glance in my direction. "I forgot to tell you she was coming. She called yesterday, but..."

"You got distracted," I said flatly.

"Honestly, I forgot myself until she arrived last night. I'm sorry that you found out that way."

"Every woman loves finding a beautiful, naked sociopath in their house in the morning." I moved away from him, rifling through the cabinet and pulling out various tea tins. I popped the lids off each until the floral, astringent scent of Assam hit my nostrils. I shoved the others back inside.

Smith turned on the hob and placed the freshly-filled kettle on it. "I wouldn't call her a sociopath exactly."

"That's the hill you're going to die on?" I asked as I searched for a teapot. I'd become too reliant on Mrs. Winters the last few weeks, so much so that I barely knew my own kitchen.

He found it first and placed it on a silver breakfast tray along with a gold-rimmed cup and saucer. Smith didn't say anything as I shifted my attention toward the fridge.

"Let me," he said when I turned with butter and marmalade in my hands.

I watched as my husband toasted a slice of bread, waiting for him to fill me in on the details of our unexpected guest. Instead, he focused on making my toast with the intensity of a Michelin-starred chef. He still hadn't spoken when the kettle whistled. I picked it up off the hob using a kitchen towel and poured the boiling water into my waiting teapot. The team bloomed in the steaming water, releasing the promising smell of comfort, but today it only turned my stomach.

"How long is she going to be here?" I demanded as I placed the pot on the tray. It was bad enough that I'd had witnesses to my mental breakdown. Now we were adding another. Georgia Kincaid was far from my favorite person. Plus, there was the fact that she had other people she should be worrying about. "What about Clara? She should be with her. She needs actual protection."

My best friend had people actively working to hurt her, and they nearly had earlier this year. I was just going crazy.

It didn't matter whether I had a bodyguard if the threat was my own mind.

He put the plate of toast on the tray and turned to finally face me.

"She's going to help me look into some things. She's not here to be your babysitter." Smith placed his hands on my shoulders, angling his head so that I was forced to meet his green eyes. It was hard to look into them and see the love there. I didn't understand how he could still feel that way after what I'd done.

"What kind of things?" I added suspiciously.

"The incident in London at your baby shower. We shouldn't just forget that happened." The lie slipped so smoothly from his lips that if I didn't know my husband as well as I did, I might have believed him.

I was being handled. I could sense it. I didn't have to ask why, but I hated that he couldn't be honest with me. I shrugged out of his grip, tossing a glib remark instead of calling him on the lie. "I probably sent it to myself. Did you consider that? I mean, who knows how long I've been a mental case."

"Beautiful." His tone shifted to a deep baritone, rich with warning. It sent goosebumps rippling over my skin. "No one is allowed to talk about my wife that way, even her."

"Truth hurts, Price." I picked up the tray and walked out of the kitchen. I wasn't sticking around for him to feed me more placating words.

Smith was up to something. There was a time that I might have pressed him on the matter, but now? I no longer trusted myself. How could he trust me? I'd made up my mind to do as he asked me, which meant making a place for Georgia in my home—like it or not.

One benefit of adding more guests to Thornham was that it gave me something to do. We hadn't spent much time worried about the guest house on our new property, because we hadn't foreseen needing it. Now that Nora had moved in full-time to help with Penny, and Edward was staying, we didn't have space in the main house for the new additions.

I was less keen on having my Aunt Jane come to stay. She'd stopped by the hospital when Penny was born, cooing in baby talk and enjoying herself. It had been a lovely visit. That was before the crying started. I had barely talked to her since then. Aunt Jane, being the saint she was, must have assumed that I was simply busy with being a new mum. I'd meant to invite her for Christmas, or even call her, for that matter. Instead, like I'd done with everyone else, I'd taken to ignoring her. I didn't want anyone to know how much I was struggling. It had been hard enough when Edward showed up. Smith had made the call to her, and I didn't have the courage to ask him what he'd told her. Whatever it was, she'd dropped her New Year's plans and told us she would be here tomorrow.

"What about these?" Edward appeared carrying a box from the main house. "Lamps. Books."

I nodded and pointed for him to set it in the corner. We

could add the items once we had more furniture. "It's a start. We're going to have to go shopping though."

"Do we have to?" He feigned annoyance at the suggestion. The truth was that Edward was probably getting stir-crazy cooped up in the house all day.

"I could order things online." My lips twitched at his instant look of horror.

"You'll do no such thing," he said quickly, moving to help me finish the bed I was making up. "Besides, a day in the city would do you some good."

"We don't have to go to the city. There are shops here," I told him. It wasn't as though Briarshead was without anything to do.

"I'm pretending you didn't say that," he said. "We can go next week. They can live with it as it is for now."

I looked around the space and frowned. The guesthouse had two bedrooms—a good thing, since I couldn't imagine asking Jane and Georgia to share a room without killing each other—plus a small kitchen and a living space. It might be nice if we'd seen to it at all in advance. I hardly felt like I was playing the gracious hostess by asking anyone to stay here. With Mrs. Winters help, we managed to pull together enough bedding to see that there was a place for them to sleep. We'd managed to have new beds delivered from the shops, which meant I wouldn't stumble in on Georgia in the buff in the morning but we hadn't been able to procure much else in the sandwiched days between Christmas and New Year.

"I wish he told me she was coming," I muttered.

"It's not like that. He didn't know until..." It wasn't like

Edward to take Smith's side and I shot him a look. He shifted gears immediately. "But he should have told you."

"It's just..." I bit my lip. There was no point in dwelling on it. What was done was done, and I needed to focus on what needed to happen next.

"You'll feel better if you tell me." Edward took a seat on the bed and patted the spot next to him.

I joined him. "It's just that I don't want people to see me like this."

"See you like what?"

"Scared. Useless." I closed my eyes and muttered the worst of all, "Crazy."

"You aren't crazy," Edward said, grabbing my hand. "You're just going through a lot right now. So much has happened to you in the last two years."

"It shouldn't be this hard, though," I confessed to him. "I wanted a baby. I got the baby. I have a husband who loves me. I have this amazing house. I have a household staff, for fuck's sake—and I can't keep my shit together."

"I'm the Prince of England and I can keep my shit together," he sympathized. "Look, none of us expect you to have all the answers. We just want to help."

"I guess I just wish I didn't need it." That was the real problem. It had been a struggle to get myself to the point of going to the doctor to ask for medicine. Medicine that hadn't worked. Tea that hadn't worked. Then I failed to even nurse Penny. But none of that compared to the most unforgivable act of all: putting her in danger. I'd only held her a few times since yesterday morning, and only in the presence of someone else. Smith had stayed true to his promise. If Nora wasn't around, he stayed close by, switching shifts with Edward to speak to Georgia. Someone was always there. I needed a nanny more than my daughter. "I'm scared to even touch her."

"Do you remember anything about yesterday morning?" Edward asked softly.

It was the first time anyone has asked me about what happened. Smith seemed too scared to go there, and I couldn't. Nora, despite how good she was with the baby, seemed to lack the maturity to acknowledge anything had happened at all. Mrs. Winters continued on like it was a normal day but kept plying me with more freaking tea. The only person that seemed willing to hold me accountable and hear my confession was Edward.

"I remember lying down. That's it." The rest was a cold, white haze until Smith called my name.

"Do you remember coming to get the baby from me?"

I shook my head.

He hung his own in shame. "I should've realized something was wrong. I'm sorry."

"You should be able to trust a child with her mother," I said fiercely. The too familiar ache of tears swelled in my throat. I didn't have the energy to fight them. Thankfully, Edward never seemed to judge me when I started to cry. Instead, he wrapped his strong arm around my shoulder and pulled me close. It took me a moment to realize that he was crying, too.

"We're a pair, aren't we?" He said hollowly. "The prince who fell for the villain —"

"And his mental case best friend," I added.

Edward didn't try to argue with me. He seemed to understand that sometimes the best thing anyone can do to help a friend is let them confront their fears. He gave me a safe space to face who I saw in the mirror and what I feared I was becoming. I didn't need someone to tell me I wasn't crazy. Right now, I was struggling to accept that I was. Most of the time I felt normal. But facts were facts, and I endangered Penny on that ice. I had been struggling since she came home to keep on top of everything. Right now, I seemed normal. Capable even. But I couldn't help dreading the next time one of those moods took hold. What would happen then?

Or even worse, whom would I hurt?

"I got a call from Tomas," Edward said suddenly.

I swiped at my tears and found myself smiling despite everything. "He likes you."

"I doubt there's many bachelors on the market here," Edward said with more than a little self-deprecation. "He's probably just desperate."

"Yes, forcing himself to be interested in a handsome, funny, intelligent Prince. He really should have higher standards."

"I thought we were being nihilistic" Edward pointed out.

I gave him an apologetic smile. He was better at this best friend thing than I was.

"You can see yourself however you want," I told him, "but don't pretend that that cute guy is looking for a pity date when he calls you."

"Okay, then, is this the part where I point out that Smith adores you more than ever?" he asked.

"Let's focus on Tomas," I said quickly. "I'll do a better job feeding your self-loathing. I don't know what he sees in you. I can't believe he called—but what did he say?"

"That's better." Edward grinned. "He's having a dinner party at the Briar Rose for New Year's Eve. He invited us."

"I don't know if I'm up for a party," I admitted.

"I thought you might say that," Edward said. "I told him I would only come if you were there."

"No! You should go," I jumped in, realizing my mistake too late.

"Sorry. We're a package deal."

"You don't want to drag along your sad sack best friend on a date with a hot French chef," I told him.

"It's not a date," he said in a quiet voice, making me regret my choice of words. "He was just being nice."

I clamped my mouth shut, knowing that this was about so much more than self-esteem issues. Edward wasn't ready to think about things like dating yet, and I couldn't blame him. But even hanging out with a hot, single guy seemed like a step in the right direction. "I don't think I should leave Smith alone on New Year's. It is sorta our anniversary."

We'd eloped in New York two years ago, but our friends had surprised us weeks later with a second wedding during a New Year's Eve party. It had also felt more like our real anniversary to me, because everything about it reminded me of the power of a fresh start. Smith had been where my life had truly begun. He was the beginning of everything for me.

"He's invited," Edward said, looking at me like this was obvious.

"Who is watching the baby?"

"You're the one with a household staff," he reminded me. "And your aunt will be here by then."

"When my aunt hears there's a dinner party, she's going to expect an invitation. Just take her with you." I couldn't imagine asking Jane to skip a party to change nappies. I wasn't even sure if she knew how to change nappies, come to think of it.

"Belle, it's okay for you to do something normal." The hesitation in his voice sounded like I wasn't the only one he was trying to convince.

Maybe he was right. "I'll talk to Smith. I'm not sure he'll go for it."

"He's going to have to take a risk someday," Edward said.

"Maybe." I couldn't help but wonder if that were true. When it came to his family, Smith Price wasn't inclined to gamble—and, in the last few days, I'd made him even more protective. There was no way he would leave Penny for that long with just Nora. Edward would go to New Year's with Jane, and we'd stay here to serve our sentence. I needed to get used to being a prisoner in my own house as much as my own mind. It wasn't a choice I had made. It was simply the way things had to be.

6

SMITH

Belle's aunt arrived in a flurry of silk and fur and energy that reminded me of the chaotic pace of the city we'd left behind. Belle had been apprehensive about the choice to invite her, worried that the house was reaching maximum capacity. But there was something about Jane that made it impossible to feel negative in her presence. I'd filled her in on what had happened at Thornham, but she'd acted completely normally since her arrival. She was exactly what my wife needed.

"Your Feng Shui is all wrong in this room," she announced as Belle and I gave her a tour of the estate. "We'll have to fix that. You'll sleep better."

Belle rolled her eyes over her aunt's shoulder, but the wide smile that accompanied her reaction spoke volumes to how she really felt.

"Whatever you need," I said. "Just tell me where to move things."

"I do like a man who's willing to jump in and get a little

sweaty." Jane nudged Belle in the rib with her elbow. "I hope you put him to work often."

There was no mistaking the double entendre in her words. I took that as a sign to excuse myself to my study. "I'm sure you two want to catch up," I said. "I have a few matters to attend to. Call if you need me?"

I leaned over to kiss Belle, but she turned her head slightly. She was still a little upset with me for turning the estate into a boarding house. But I couldn't help thinking the more normalcy I could give her, the better. We were used to being surrounded by friends and family. Perhaps, surrounding her with people now would help her feel more like her old self.

There were plenty of things to attend to in my study. Bills to be paid. Calls to be returned. I'd put opening the law firm on an indefinite hold while we sorted through what was going on in the house.

Georgia was in my study when I entered, feet propped up on my desk, leaning back in my chair and studying what appeared to be my files.

"Make yourself at home," I said dryly.

"I did." She didn't bother to look up from the file folder in her hands.

"Anything interesting?"

"I think so." She closed the folder and placed it back on the desk. Georgia leaned and crossed her arms on its surface, leveling her dark gaze at me. "I was looking at the names of the people that were interviewed after the disappearance and I found some curious coincidences. What's the name of your housekeeper again?"

"Fuck, I was afraid you'd say something like that," I muttered, circling around the desk to pick up the folder she'd been looking at.

Georgia leaned over and rifled through the papers until she landed on a particular report from the police interviews. "Winters."

"She's not that old," I said. "It couldn't be her."

"No," Georgia agreed. "But what if her family worked here before? Did she mention it?"

I frowned. "It's hardly an unusual name."

"Maybe." That seemed to be Georgia's newest noncommittal response. *Maybe.* But I didn't need her to commit to more. I knew exactly what she was thinking without her having to say it directly. We've seen too much in our years to believe in things like coincidence.

"What else?"

"The rest of your staff," she said, moving more folders on my desk to show she'd been looking through the employee files. "All of them had family who worked here, except Rowan and Nora."

"So two of them? That's hardly a conspiracy."

"Hold up a sec, Price. Nora has no connection to Thornham. She's young. A college student."

"I've met her," I reminded Georgia.

"But Rowan," Georgia continued, without acknowledging my insertion, "he worked here."

"I think I knew that." I screwed up my memory trying to keep straight what had been said during interviews. "He's only one old enough to have worked here. I remember it coming up."

"That's good," Georgia murmured absently, moving his file to the other side of the desk.

"I don't really see what this has to do with our problems."

"I just find it odd that you've got a household staff full of people with connections to the original owners."

"I doubt there's a lot of jobs available locally for people in their lines of work," I pointed out. "I hardly think that means they're out to get me. Besides, I don't know any of them. Why would they come after us?"

"Maybe someone asked them to."

Georgia hadn't given up on her concern that this might be linked to MI-18. She'd brought it up a number of times since her arrival, and despite having no evidence to support her theory, she seemed more convinced than ever. With anyone else I might have written this off as paranoia. But Georgia wasn't prone to overreaction. She was always the one who managed to keep things on an even keel. Something about this situation bothered her on a visceral level. Truthfully, it bothered me, too. It scratched in the back of mine like a stray, unwanted but determined to get inside. Both of us were far too rational to think there wasn't an explanation for all the madness. We had enough enemies in our past, the last thing we were worried about was a house turning on us.

"What are you two doing for your anniversary?" Georgia asked.

I looked at her in surprise. "It's not really our anniversary."

"Word to the wise, never say the words 'it's not really

our anniversary' to anyone again," she said. "Especially your wife. Just buy her flowers."

"There's nothing to do in the village. I'm sure people around her just hit the pubs."

"Edward told me about a dinner party," she said. "You two should go."

This was news to me. Why hadn't Belle mentioned it?

"I don't feel comfortable leaving Penny here without one of us," I admitted. "I'm sure Nora would do just fine. I just..."

I couldn't put my finger on it. As much as I appreciated the staff. I didn't know any of them. I couldn't trust them the way I could trust myself or Edward or Georgia.

"You need to get her out of this house."

She might have a point. It was obviously a coincidence that Belle's problems began when we moved here full time. But that didn't mean that getting her away from those problems—even for a night—wouldn't do her some good. "I'll make her go with Jane and Edward. It will be good for her."

"You should be with her," Georgia said. "Anniversary, remember?"

"Someone has to stay with the baby, and I want you to go with them and keep an eye on things."

"No dice." Georgia shook her head and pushed back from the desk. "I'll stay with the baby."

"You'll... What?" I'd heard her wrong. There was no way that Georgia Kincaid had just offered to babysit.

"I'm around a baby all the time," she said defensively. "I won't break it."

"Her," I said gently. "You just don't seem the motherly type."

"Neither do you," she snapped. "Look, I can change a nappy. I can give a bottle. I'm not totally useless."

"Are those really the new criteria now?" Belle's cold voice cut in.

"Beautiful," I said, whirling toward her and finding her standing with Jane just inside the door. "Georgia just offered to stay with Nora and Penny on New Year's so that we could go out." Georgia cleared her throat lightly, and I added, "for our anniversary."

"You want to stay with our baby?" Belle's surprise mirrored my own reaction.

Georgia looked even more put out. "You know, the Queen of England trusts me with her kid, so maybe you two could lower your standards just a little."

"I didn't know that you liked kids," Belle said quickly, clearly worried that she had offended her.

"I don't."

We all waited for her to finish that statement, but she didn't.

"If you're sure," I said, eyeing her to see if she was just being polite.

It was Jane that finally interrupted, "Oh Lord, just take the help. Penny will be in good hands. And I want to go dancing and I want to see you two dancing."

Belle and I shared a sheepish look. That would require us putting our little disagreement behind us. I didn't want to force her to forgive me because of some holiday. "Sounds good to me. If you want me to come, beautiful?"

I put it in her hands. I told myself that if she said she didn't want me there it didn't mean anything, except that she wanted to relax and be with her friends. But when she finally nodded, relief washed through me.

"Then it's settled." Jane clapped her hands. "A new year always reminds me that there's not enough time to wait for the perfect moment. There's only time to live."

I found myself hoping she was right.

7

BELLE

"I have nothing to wear," I announced, coming out of my closet. I'd been in there for the last ten minutes shoving apart hangers and staring at dozens of choices. Nothing felt right.

"You have half of Harrods in there." Edward strode past me into the closet and turned, planting his hands on his hips. He was already dressed in his outfit for the evening. Most years we wound up doing something that required tuxedos, but this year, given that we were going to a dinner party in the village, that seemed like overkill. That left me not knowing what to wear. Edward, as always, knew exactly how to rise to the challenge. He'd opted for a pair of well tailored charcoal trousers, a polished pair of Testoni loafers and a thickly knit sweater, its toggle button open at the neck to reveal a hint of the pressed white shirt below. He looked effortlessly effortlessly casual with his dark curls artfully combed away from his clean-shaven face. "You have one million things to wear in here."

I followed him inside, shaking my head. "All of these were from before."

"You have an expiration date for clothes now? Belle, you run a fashion empire," he reminded me.

How could I explain to him that I felt differently now. "None of it will look the same. Nothing is where it used to be." I waved a hand over my body, hoping he would get the picture. My boobs were still bigger than before Penny. My stomach softer. My hips fuller.

"You look fabulous," he said, dismissing my concern.

"I don't feel it," I said softly. I rolled my eyes. "Just pick something for me."

"I never thought the day would come that I got to dress you." He looked as if I just handed him a belated Christmas gift.

"Fine, but nothing too flashy." I didn't want to draw attention to myself in the village tonight. Who knew what rumors were going around about the Prices and Thornham. He shooed me out of the closet.

"Be patient, and you will see how genius creates a legend," he called to me.

"Legend? We think awfully highly of ourselves."

His curly head popped out, plastered with a smug grin. "I'm royalty, remember?"

I sat down on the edge of the bed and began chewing my fingernails nervously. I still wasn't sure about leaving Penny, even with Georgia here. But neither Smith nor Edward seemed willing to let me back out of the evening's plans. I also didn't have a leg to stand on. Given that I had been avoiding being alone with the baby, it seemed strange to insist on staying with her now. For some reason though, it felt like a bad idea. Then again, given my mental state, maybe I wasn't the best person to make this decision.

Edward appeared from the closet a few minutes later, holding a dress bag. He smiled triumphantly as he held up. "Legend, I tell you."

I stared at the black bag as I tried to remember what was inside.

"It's perfect, and you're going to look smashing," he told me as he placed it across the bad. Edward unzipped the bag carefully to reveal a deep blue dress. It's color was so dark it nearly looked black. Even on the hanger, I could see he was right. Sheer sleeves tapered to elegant sequined cuffs and its long, portrait-style neck in the same light chiffon allowed it to gracefully skim the very edge of where my shoulders would be before dipping into an open back. Its bodice was simple until it reached the waistline where sequins formed an erratic, but sophisticated pattern that accentuated the curve of the hips. From there scattered sequins fell like dark stars along the fabric to its floor-length hemline.

"I don't remember buying this," I said, fingering it's sleeve. "It was probably from one of Bless's designers. Isn't it a little too dressy?"

"Honestly, I hang around with people who have to wear tuxedos to birthday parties, so I may not be the best judge," he said, winking at me, "but I think it's perfect."

"I'll try it on." I wasn't ready to commit to it just yet. I excused myself to the loo to change. From the moment, I slipped into the dress, I knew he'd chosen correctly. I felt like myself for the first time in ages. There was no huge baby bump changing the way it looked on me. It wasn't trousers and a sweater meant for mucking around the property. It was elegant and sophisticated and sexy—exactly what I wanted to wear to bring in the new year. But I wasn't ever going to be the woman I'd been before. Wearing a dress couldn't change that. Maybe I needed to pick something more suitable to my life at Thornham and leave London Belle behind moving forward.

Edward tapped on the bathroom door, and I opened it. His eyes scanned me before he let out a low whistle. "You're going to wind up pregnant again if you wear that."

"In that case, I'm changing." I pushed past him, but he caught my wrist.

"I'm only joking. You look amazing."

I bit my lip and stared questioningly at him. "I don't know up from down anymore."

He spun me around to look in the mirror, standing behind me. Edward rested his hands on my shoulders and leaned down, lowering his voice. "You're still you. No matter what changes. Even when it's you that's changing, it's okay to hold on to some bits."

My hand reached up and squeezed his. I didn't trust myself to say anything. Most of the time, I didn't feel like me. I didn't feel like anyone. And it was stupid that a dress could somehow get me closer to the person I remembered being. It gave me hope that maybe she was still in there somewhere.

"Let's get your hair done," he said, reaching to pull it up. "I think you should show off your neck. It's so graceful, just like a swan."

"I'm glad I know you're gay or I might think you were hitting on my wife," a gruff voice broke in. I peeked over Edward's shoulder, angling myself carefully behind him so Smith couldn't see what I'd chosen to wear. Smith himself had opted for a dark blue suit. One of the ones he used to wear at his offices in London. I'd always loved it. Off the top of my head, I could think of a half-dozen times he fucked me wearing that suit. My toes curled against the tiles under my feet. Maybe Edward was right. Maybe we had to find the parts of us we wanted to keep and cling to them.

Still, we couldn't ignore the things that were changing. That's why Smith was having hushed conversations with Georgia behind closed doors and why my aunt had been called to intervene. How could we hold on to each other when we were being torn apart?

"I'm almost ready." I reached around Edward and shut the bathroom door. The last thing I saw was a glimpse of Smith's stunned face as it slammed shut.

Edward chuckled under his breath. "What's up with you two?"

"That's a long story," I said with a sigh. "He's keeping secrets. But I know what he's not saying. He thinks I'm broken."

"*He* thinks that?" Edward said meaningfully.

"He thinks it. I know it," I murmured softly. "And does that change anything between you two?"

"Shouldn't it?" It was the very question I've been pondering for the last few days. "How can Smith still look at me with love in his eyes after what I did? How can he trust me? I don't trust me! How does love survive that?"

"No," Edward said in a firm, but quiet voice. "True love can't be broken."

"Even when people are broken?" I whispered.

"Especially when people are broken. That's when love's the strongest, because it's made from the parts that survived the breaking," he said. He squeezed my shoulders. "Now what are we going to do about your hair?"

A half hour later my hair was pinned into an elegant twist, I had a fresh set of false lashes applied courtesy of my best friend and my lips were painted crimson red. I hand't felt this sexy in a long time. Despite the awkwardness between me and Smith, I found a La Perla garter in my closet and shimmied it on along with silk stockings. Maybe a little champagne would give me the courage to tempt him with a peek at them.

"My work here is done." Edward said when I came back out of the closet. "Legend."

"Pretty good." I steadied myself against the door frame and slipped on a pair of silver Louboutins.

He rolled his eyes. "I'm going to make sure they're heating up the cars. See you downstairs?"

I nodded. There were still a few things I needed to do. I made sure that I had everything I needed in a small Chanel clutch before I left the bedroom. Part of me wanted to go downstairs and avoid the nursery altogether. The part of me that was sure I didn't deserve to be Penny's mother. But since this was going to be one of the first nights I had away from my baby, I found myself heading there anyway. When

I peeked inside, I found Nora rocking a sleeping Penny against her chest. Georgia had taken the other upholstered chair in the room, swinging her legs over the side, while scrolling on her phone. It wasn't the picture of domestic bliss I'd anticipated when I decorated the nursery. Then, I'd expected to sit long hours in the blush pink room, an extra chair next to mine for Smith to join us. We would be a family cut straight from a catalog page. I couldn't have been more wrong.

Nora's eyes flickered up and met mine. She smiled softly, and I took that as a sign that I was welcome to come in. It was strange to think that I felt I needed permission to be near my own child, but that's how the last few days have been. I tiptoed inside, worried that I would wake her. When I reached the glider, I hesitated for only a second before leaning down to kiss the downy hair on her head.

"Have a good time tonight," Nora whispered.

I swallowed, forcing myself to nod before turning to Georgia.

"You know how to reach us."

She did a good job of not acting offended by this statement. Instead, she tipped her head. "We'll be fine."

"Still..." In truth, we both knew that Penny was better off here with the two of them than with me tonight. But it felt like it was my job to show concern over leaving her.

It wasn't that I didn't want to be here. I couldn't imagine a better way to spend the start of the new year than cuddling my daughter next to the room's crackling fireplace with Smith at my side. But what if I had another episode? I couldn't risk it. It was better this way.

I backed out of the room, my eyes never leaving Penny's curled-up form. Nora had dressed her in a white-smocked one piece with a Peter Pan collar. Together, the two of them looked almost angelic. Penny, a bright light and Nora, her dark protector. A bitter taste filled my mouth, and I turned away, leaving the nursery behind. This was supposed to be my life, but it didn't feel like my own anymore. I should be grateful to Nora for taking care of my daughter when I couldn't be trusted. Instead, I felt nothing but jealousy. I stopped a moment in the hallway to collect myself, straightening my shoulders and preparing to put on a cheerful face for everyone downstairs.

As I descended the staircase, Smith walked into view and stopped at the landing. His eyes met mine and the look of love there stole my breath away. I clutched the railing, feeling myself tremble under the weight of his gaze and somehow managed to make it to the bottom.

"You're beautiful," he said simply.

"So you're always telling me," I said with a shrug.

He hooked an arm around my waist and drew me to him. Smith tipped my chin up with his index finger, his green eyes piercing through me. "Don't do that. Don't make yourself less than you are."

"And what am I?" I breathed.

"Everything." His face angled over mine, leaning to capture a kiss. It was slow and full of unspoken things—the words we hadn't said the last few days. Suddenly, I knew that Edward was right. None of what happened mattered to Smith. He would stand by me no matter what. I might not deserve him, but I wasn't about to let him go. In his arms, his mouth pressed to mine, his tongue licking a hungry line across the roof of my mouth, I remembered that I belonged to him. He would protect me. If I was broken, he would put me back together. When he finally broke away, he pressed his forehead against mine and whispered, "We could just stay in..."

"I was promised champagne and dancing," I reminded him.

"Well, in that case." He offered me his arm, and I took it.

"Where are the others?" We paused at the door and he wrapped a mink stole around my shoulders.

"I sent them ahead. I wanted a few minutes alone with my wife." He glanced over at me, an unreadable expression passing over his face. "Is that okay with you?"

"I always want a moment with you." It was the truth. It was what we needed. I could see that now. I'd been so keen on punishing myself that I lost sight of what really mattered. We had something worth fighting for. Our love. Our family. We would make it through this.

"Are you ready, Mrs. Price?" he asked, his question suddenly taking on a whole new meaning.

"Lead the way, Mr. Price."

8

BELLE

The Christmas snow had lingered all week, and it seemed we were in for a white New Year as well. Plump snowflakes fell against the dark sky as we drove toward Briarshead. I missed the Bugatti, but as the Range Rover's tires crunched along the snow-strewn roads, I found myself realizing Smith had been right about the larger vehicle. My hand was in Smith's, resting on its large leather console, as we made our way to celebrate a new beginning. When we arrived in the village, there were crowds of boisterous partygoers crawling between the town's three pubs.

"Shit." Smith surveyed the crowds and cast a worried look at me. "Not exactly what I was expecting."

"I doubt they're going to head to the Briar Rose." In fact, I knew they wouldn't be. According to Edward, Tomas had closed the restaurant for tonight's party "It's by invitation only. I don't think we have to worry about drunk university students."

By the time we reached the end of the high street, the crowds had dissipated. We found the Briar Rose lit up warmly with strings of party bulbs on the outside. Through the windows we could see groups of people milling around. I spotted Jane speaking animatedly with a man half her age. I had no doubt she'd have him seduced by midnight.

Inside, the Briar Rose had been transformed from a cozy, if eclectic, British tavern into a swanky club for the evening. The lights were dim, the lanterns hanging from the ceiling flickering romantically overhead. Large bouquets of white roses clustered on every table with feather plumes sticking out of them, adding to the atmosphere of the fête. The tables had been laid with white linen cloth and set formally with gold rimmed, bone china and silver. In the center of the room a large tower of coupe glasses had been erected just waiting for champagne to overflow from the glass on top. Rather than have servers, the bar had been turned into a buffet of mouth watering delicacies. I was already eyeing what looked to be a platter of foie gras when Jane accosted us at the door. She thrust a glass of champagne into my hands and leaned to kiss me on the cheek.

"Are you ready for the new year?" she asked.

The sip of champagne I'd started to take turned into a gulp, and I nodded with wide eyes. This year had been full of too many ups and downs. From the incredible high of expecting our first child and then welcoming her into the world to the terrible events that had hurt so many people I loved, I was more than ready for the clock to strike midnight.

Jane had chosen a loose-fitting, sequined gown that hung off her shoulders. A woman in her twenties wouldn't be able to wear it with the amount of sophistication and confidence that my aunt could. She owned the dress, and by the end of the night, I suspected she'd own every heart in the room.

"If you'll excuse me," Smith said, "I'm going to get you something to eat, beautiful." He disappeared toward the bar before I could stop him.

"You really picked a good one." Jane sighed as her eyes traveled along after him. "Now help me pick one."

"You're looking for a husband?" I asked with a raised eyebrow.

Jane swatted my arm, laughing merrily as if I'd made a good joke. "Oh no, I have no interest in giving up my freedom now. Ones like him don't come along every day. Just remember that." She paused, a look of distant pain flashing over her face. I knew the truth. Jane had found the right one and lost him. She married a handful of times, the relationships each lasted such a short while that she'd told me herself they didn't count.

"Are you okay?" I asked in a lowered voice. I knew all too well how easy it was to lock away pain.

"Don't fuss over me," she said, instantly brightening. "I love my life. I'm completely happy by myself. That's the trick, you know," she lowered her voice conspiratorially. "Whether you're single or you're married, love yourself wildly and you will always be happy."

"I'll keep that in mind," I promised her. "So, what am I picking out for you then?"

"I'm not a nun. I may love myself, but I don't mind enjoying loving someone else in bed every now and then," she said with a wink.

Since Jane was sharing the guest house with Georgia, I wondered how it would go down if she took a man home tonight. Then again, I wasn't about to stop her. It wasn't as if I could if I wanted to.

"What about him?" I tilted my head toward a man with salt-and-pepper hair and a graying beard. He was dressed in an expensive suit and sipping a glass of bourbon. Perhaps, he felt my eyes on him, because he looked up and smiled widely when he saw me standing there with Jane. "Very handsome," she agreed, "but he's looking for a wife."

And Jane clearly wasn't looking for a husband. I nodded in understanding. "That young chef is tasty," she said in a low voice, "but I fear his heart is spoken for."

I followed her gaze to where Tomas and Edward were talking, standing a little more closely than friends might. Edward said something and Tomas laughed, touching his arm lightly.

"I'm afraid that Tomas might be disappointed," I murmured. Just getting Edward to go out was a step in the right direction, but I knew he wasn't ready for a relationship. Still, it was good to see him talking with someone.

"It will take some time," Jane agreed. "But in my experience, that doesn't mean you have to be celibate."

I laughed. "I'll make sure to remind him of that."

"Please do." She continued to scan the room for prospects. Her hand tightened over my wrist as another man, bearing a striking resemblance to Tomas, entered the restaurant. "Well, hello."

She licked her coral lipstick. Apparently, her evening's target had been acquired.

"I think I'll find Smith." She didn't need my help when it came to flirting.

Jane nodded absently, still watching the new arrival. "I think I'll play hostess. Tomas seems otherwise engaged."

Within seconds, she was across the room, her smile sparkling as much as her dress as she welcomed the man to the party. He must be related to Tomas. They looked too similar. But this man was slightly older. He had to have a good twenty to twenty-five years on him. I made a mental note to ask about him when I finally had a moment with my new friend.

Smith joined me, holding a plate of hors d'oeuvres, and I plucked a tiny piece of toast topped with foie gras from it. "Thank you."

"I knew what you wanted, beautiful," he said with a smile.

"Am I that predictable?" I asked.

"No, I just know you." His eyes smoldered into mine and I took my time taking a bite, allowing it to linger near my lips, imagining what would come later. Smith's gaze danced over my mouth as I savored the delicate hors d'oeuvre. As soon as its rich, buttery taste spread across my tongue, I closed my eyes and moaned with pleasure.

"You're making me jealous," he said in the lowered voice. "I'm supposed to be the one that makes you moan like that."

"Consider it foreplay, Price." I said, following the delicacy with a coy sip of champagne.

"There you are," Edward called, moving to join us.

I looked around for Tomas but found he'd gone to greet the gentleman that Jane had zeroed in on. The three of them were standing in a corner, chatting as if they'd all known each other for years. "Who is that?"

"His uncle," Edward told me. "He owns a vineyard or something in France."

"But he came here for New Year's?"

"I guess fate has plans for him," Edward said wryly as we watched Jane flirtatiously place a hand on the man's coat jacket.

"Fate or Aunt Jane," Smith muttered. "I'm not sure which is a stronger force of nature."

"It's Jane," Edward and I said at the same time.

"Everything looks beautiful," I said to Edward.

"Wait until you see the menu."

Edward's proclamation proved true. I'd been impressed by my other experiences with Briar Rose, but it was nothing compared to this evening's feast. Tomas had leaned into his French heritage to produce one of the best meals I'd ever had in my life. Somehow, even though we were all clustered next to each other in the room, the whole affair felt intimate. Courses were served family style to each table.

The hors d'oeuvres had been a taste of what was to come. More foie gras and fresh baguettes were delivered to the tables along with buttery escargot. Smith and I took turns scooping the tiny delicacies from their shells and feeding them to each other. Two main courses followed, a whole Scottish salmon served with a creamy béarnaise and a braised leg of lamb resting on steamed haricots verts. Each bite was more sinful than the last, made all the better by how much hungrier Smith's eyes became as the evening progressed.

His hand slid to rest on the small of my back as we talked and laughed with our friends. Jane had Hughes, Tomas's uncle, completely enraptured. It was a perfect night. When a platter of profiteroles and fresh strawberries were placed in front of us with a steaming pot of melted French chocolate to dip them into, I wasn't sure I could eat another bite.

"I think I'm too full," I whispered to Smith. But he'd already picked up a strawberry and dipped it into the chocolate. "Just one for me, beautiful."

He brought it to my mouth and pushed it gently past my lips. My teeth sank into it, my eyes never leaving his as the tart sweetness of strawberry mixed with rich dark chocolate on my tongue. This was definitely becoming foreplay.

"Do you want to stay until midnight?" he asked in a husky voice.

"Do you have something else in mind?" I asked, feigning innocence.

"I can think of several ways I'd like to ring in the new year with you." He brought his lips to my ear, brushing the stubble on his chin across the sensitive skin of my neck. "But one dance first."

I nodded, lost to words, too intoxicated by the man next to me to think of a thing to say. My thoughts were already racing forward to being alone with him. Deep inside me, my core clenched in anticipation as he stood and offered me his hand. There was no traditional dance floor in the Briar Rose, but a few couples had pressed close together to sway to the jazzy music playing on the stereo. As we stood it shifted to a more bluesy rift, and I found myself laughing when I recognized the Rolling Stones. "They're playing our song."

"I know," Smith said with a devilish grin as he swept me into his arms.

"You're full of surprises tonight, Price." I wrapped my arms around his neck.

"I guess I always feel romantic on our anniversary," he murmured as I laid my head against his shoulder.

"What if I want you to be a little dirty instead?" I asked him.

"I think I can manage both. As you said, I'm full of surprises, and, beautiful, you're going to be full of me soon."

I felt the bulge of his erection press into my belly as if to prove the point. He bent to whisper in my ear. "I will never have enough of you. This year. Next year. Every year."

It was perfect. The beginning that I wanted. Here with him, belonging to him, remembering our past but moving forward together. Nothing could tear us apart like the song said. When it's final bars faded away, Smith looked down at me. "Should we say or should we go?"

"I think I'm ready for you to show me how you want to ring in the new year," I told him, lowering my lashes flirtatiously.

"I'll warm up the car." Before he could move towards the door, he leaned and kissed me full on the lips. My mouth parted in welcome, a happy sigh escaping me as he pulled away with a smirk. "Consider that a sneak preview."

I made my way back to our table to find my wrap and my clutch, scanning the room to say goodbye. Jane and Hughes were tucked in a corner, their heads close together talking. I hated to interrupt them. Instead, my eyes found Edward. He had just finished a dance with Tomas and gone to the bar to get another glass of wine. Maneuvering my way through the crowd, I joined him. Before I could stop him, he poured a glass for me, too. "Actually, we're leaving."

Edward frowned, his eyes narrowing in concern. "Are you feeling okay?"

"I think we just want to be alone," I said, biting my lip. It occurred to me that maybe I should stay with my best friend, so he didn't have to face the new year alone. But Edward didn't seem concerned over my departure, instead he gave me a swift kiss and a smile. "In that case, happy early new year."

I tapped my glass against his in a toast. "To a new start."

"To a new start," he echoed. I saw the same hope I felt in his eyes. This year had to be better than the last one for both of us. I downed the drink quickly as Smith reappeared in the doorway.

"I think your Prince Charming has arrived," Edward said with a grin.

I wouldn't consider Smith my Prince Charming. He was my dark knight, my savior, my protector, and my haven. At his hands, I'd found the beautiful pleasure darkness could bring. I found myself in places I'd never expected to go. And even now, walking through this shadowed path with him, I knew. He might not be a Prince Charming, but he was my happily ever after.

9

SMITH

Belle's hand stayed in mine as I drove through the wintery streets of Briarshead. The village was still filled with boisterous celebration, drunken crowds weaving with pint glasses, singing off the new with exuberance. The festive atmosphere faded along with the village as we took the country road that wound to our estate.

"It's lovely," she murmured watching the snowflakes fall out the window.

"I was thinking the same thing." I raised her clasped hands and kissed the back of hers.

"I wish we didn't have to go home," she admitted in a soft voice.

"Beautiful," I began, searching for the words that might remind her that the darkness would pass. It always had before. But I didn't want to color this evening with its shadow, so I pasted a cocky grin on my face. "I thought you wanted me to take you home to ring in the new year."

Belle twisted in her seat, dropping her free hand over

my groin. She brushed the bulge there and my dick leapt to attention. "I do want to ring in the new year—with you. Only you."

There was no mistaking the invitation behind her words. We were halfway to Thornham with few other properties nearby. The road showed no signs of other cars in the freshly fallen snow. It seemed we were among the few who had bothered to leave the comforts of their home for the holiday. We were alone, and it had been a long time since I'd had Belle entirely to myself. Turning the wheel, I pulled the car off the road near a small grove of trees. "Let's not go home, then."

I left the lights on and the engine running to ensure the cabin stayed warm and we could enjoy the winter scene outside. My wife bit her crimson-stained lip, her eyes fluttering as though a dozen wicked thoughts had just flown through her head. I reached down and put my seat back before crossing my arms behind my head to relax. It wasn't an invitation or an order. I'd seen exactly what she wanted in her eyes, and I was more than happy to give it to her. Belle unfastened her safety belt and gathered her skirt so she could kneel in her seat. Her expert fingers had my trousers undone and my zipper down in seconds. She pulled my cock out, wrapping her soft fingers around it, and pumped the shaft as she lowered her lips to its crest. My eyes closed, savoring the pop of her lips over its tip and the velvet heat of her mouth wrapping around me. She took her time, stroking my shaft as she licked and sucked. I felt my balls tighten, but this time I was prepared.

I lifted her head away to find her lipstick smeared

under her lower lip and her cheeks flushed with excitement. "Part of me wants to finish the job," I told her in a low voice. "I wouldn't mind seeing that perfect face of yours covered in me. You'd like that, wouldn't you? Tell me how much you want to feel it on your skin, dripping down your neck."

"Please, sir," she whispered, her words panting from her.

"Not yet," I said and her face fell. "I want to fuck you first."

Her eyelids shuddered at the promise of my words, then she started to push up on the console. I placed my index finger on her lips. "No. Sit in your seat and be patient."

Belle returned to the leather seat and I opened my car door, not bothering to stuff my cock pack in my pants. Shrugging off my jacket, I left it in the driver's seat, knowing I wouldn't want it restricting my movement. Snowflakes hit my rock hard dick, melting on contact with the hot skin as I circled to her side of the SUV. Opening the door, I offered her my hand. She stepped carefully out, her heels sinking into the snow before I lifted her off her feet and slammed her into the side of the Range Rover. Our mouths met in a tangled collision as my hand searched for the car handle behind her. I found it and spun her carefully, so I could open it wide enough to deposit her on the backseat.

She'd lost her shoes in the snow, but she didn't seem to notice. Instead, she lifted her hips to allow me to hike the hem of her dress to her hips. I groaned when I saw the delicate lace garter holding up her sheer black stockings. It criss-crossed under her navel, forming an arrow that pointed to her bare pussy below.

"Has this been naked all night?" I asked, stroking a finger down her wet seam.

"Yes," she purred. I wasn't entirely sure if she was answering my question or if she was about to explode. I stepped between her open thighs, unable to wait any longer, sinking inside her with one deliberate thrust. Belle cried out, arching in the seat, as her legs circled my waist. Her hands reached to grab hold of my vest and she clawed up my front, bringing her lips to mine, as I drove into her. She hooked an arm around my neck so that her lips brushed lazily against mine and our eyes locked. Belle's hips circled around my cock as I rocked in and out of her, bringing us both to the edge.

Snow had managed to blow through the open door, but she showed no signs of being cold. The flakes caught in her hair and lingered for a moment before melting to glistening drops. There was no sound in the silent night except our frantic breathing and the slap of skin against skin as I fucked her under the moonlight. Belle gasped in shallow bursts and I felt her clamping over my cock, inviting me to join her. She cried out as I spilled inside her, her fingers gripping me for strength as we left the past behind us and moved forward together.

When she collapsed against me, I smiled and pressed a kiss to her forehead. "Happy New Year, beautiful." I slanted my face over hers and kissed her lips. "Any resolutions?"

"Do that more," she said in an exhausted, but content whisper.

"I think I can help with that."

I rearranged her skirt before lifting her back into the passenger's seat. Then I bent to retrieve her heels from the snow, brushing them off and tucking them near the SUV's floorboard heater.

"Thank you." She gave me a swift kiss. I closed her door, brushing wet droplets from my hair as I returned to the driver's side.

"Are you cold?" I stole a glance at my wife. Despite the weather, her cheeks were flushed from our lovemaking. A grin carved across my face when I realized I'd managed to keep her warm, even in the snow.

"Don't look so smug," she said, smacking my hand lightly.

"A man should always take pride when a wife is lit up like a full moon after he's fucked her."

"Is that right?" She leaned over the console to kiss me. Settling back into her seat, she pulled down the rearview mirror and gasped when she saw her makeup. "Lit up like the moon," she repeated. "Bollocks. I look like I was left out in the rain too long."

"Don't." I said when she went to fix the lipstick that had smeared from her lower lip. "If I promise to get you inside without anyone seeing you, will you keep it like that?"

She paused, turning from the mirror with a curious look. "Why?"

"Because it reminds me of how good you look with my

cock in your mouth," I growled. I reached over and brushed my thumb across her lower lip, smearing it more. "It makes me think of all the filthy things you can do with that mouth of yours."

"Like talk back?" she teased, but her breath caught as I pushed my thumb past her lips and dragged it over her lower teeth.

"Oh, it's a smart, pretty, little mouth," I told her. "I love everything that comes out of it—almost as much as I love putting things in it."

Belle practically vibrated as I plunged my thumb deeper inside. Her red lips closed over it, sucking it lightly.

Fuck, she was perfect. "Can't wait to have me back in your mouth can you?"

She shook her head, her eyes round saucers that shone with captured moonlight. A hand crept over the console to my lap, but I slapped it away.

"You've already had that tonight," I reminded her. "Maybe I want something in my mouth."

She whimpered, squirming in her seat. I loved seeing her like this. Loved knowing how much she still wanted it. I had so much more to give her. Tonight and every night after.

"Do you want to go home? Or should I fuck you again in the backseat?" I demanded.

Belle pulled away, running her tongue over her lower lip as if to savor the taste of my skin lingering there. Her eyes hooded lustily. "Whatever pleases you, sir."

Christ. We would be lucky to make it home tonight, at all. At least, the Range Rover had plenty of gas and heated leather seats. But before I could get back out of the car and shove her pretty little ass into the back seat, my mobile began to ring. Instantly, the air thickened around us. I pulled it from my pocket, checked the screen and answered immediately. "Is everything okay?"

Across from me, Belle's demeanor shifted in an instant. She reached for her seatbelt and strapped herself in, casting terrified glances in my direction.

"Everything is under control, but you should come home," Georgia said. "There was an incident."

"What kind of incident?" I asked, throwing the SUV into gear and pulling back onto the snow-covered road.

"Nora has had some sort of allergic reaction. Paramedics are here."

"What?" I roared.

"Everything's fine. She's fine. It was some type of misunderstanding. I figured you'd want to get home, though, since—"

"I'm on my way," I cut her off and hung up on the phone to concentrate on getting us back to the estate.

Next to me, Belle had crossed her arms over her chest protectively. She looked too scared to ask what happened.

"Nora had some type of allergic reaction," I said, trying to keep my tone as even as possible. "They had to call the paramedics."

"I didn't know she had any allergies," Belle said, looking stunned.

"Everything is under control. Georgia is there, and Penny is fine." I didn't mention that I hadn't even asked about the baby. I assumed that if something was wrong with my child, Georgia would lead with that.

Belle looked unconvinced next to me. "Smith..."

"Yes?" I asked as we raced home.

"Is anyone safe at Thornham?"

I was beginning to wonder the same thing myself.

10

BELLE

The paramedics were still there when we arrived. Smith pulled the Range Rover into the drive, and we shared a worried look.

"I think I'd better..."

"Yes," I said, sensing what he was thinking. Smith jumped out of the SUV and headed quickly toward the house. With my heels on, I was forced to take my time, carefully following him so that I wouldn't fall in the snow. Thanks to Rowan and his foresight putting down salt not much had collected. Still, I walked slowly in part to navigate the slush but also because I dreaded going inside. Every time I left Thornham, I didn't want to return. Tonight was worse than usual. I ascended the stairs, clutching the stone railing. As I got closer, I heard Penny sobbing. Panic ignited me and I dashed up the last few steps, kicked off my Louboutins in the entry, and ran up the stairs to the nursery.

I found Georgia, looking more harried than I'd ever

seen her, pacing the room while trying to comfort my daughter. Before I could think better of it, I held out my arms. "Give her to me."

Georgia didn't hesitate to pass Penny off, which either meant she trusted me more than everyone else or that she desperately wanted a break from the baby.

The moment I brought Penny to my shoulder, her crying faded to a punctuated tremble as she began to calm down. "It's okay. Mummy's here."

Relief rolled through me as I savored the feeling of my daughter in my arms. When Smith's mobile had rung on the way here, I'd known instantly something was wrong. On the drive, my mind had played a continuous reel of hypothetical accidents that could have hurt her. Nothing felt better than having her safely with me again.

Georgia crossed toward the door, and the solace I felt gave way to a sharp stab of panic.

"Don't leave me with her!"

She turned, her dark eyes flashing before she composed herself and shook her head. "She's safe with you."

"You don't know that," I said quickly. Smith wasn't here to chaperone me, and he must not have told Georgia about the arrangement.

"*I do know that.* No matter what you think, it's obvious that you would never hurt her." Her hand lingered on the doorknob as she spoke. She made no move to open it.

"You weren't there," I reminded her. "You didn't see how close I came to doing just that."

"Look, I get beating yourself up. Believe me. But you're as sane as I am. I've been watching you," she admitted to me, surprising me a bit. Georgia hadn't seemed to show much interest in me since her arrival. She was usually busy having hushed conversations with Smith or taking mysterious trips into the village. "You're going to have to believe it. Now, I really want to check on Nora. She scared me."

I hesitated, but finally nodded. I needed to face facts. Nora wouldn't be up for taking care of Penny tonight if her allergic reaction had been so bad that paramedics were called, and Georgia clearly wasn't up for the challenge. That left me either waiting for Smith or calling Edward. I looked down at Penny's content face, her big blue eyes staring up at me with wonder and realized Georgia was right. I would never do anything to hurt my child. Whatever happened that day on the ice, it had to have an explanation. Looking at Penny, I knew that I would die for her if necessary.

As soon as Georgia left, Penny began turning her head side to side, and my heart sank. She wanted to nurse. I took a deep breath and whispered to her, "We can try. But let's not get our hopes up."

Carrying her to the glider, I settled down with her. Someone had lit a fire in the hearth, and its flickering flames made the spot feel even cozier. To my surprise, she latched easily. I waited for the crying to start, watching for signs of frustration, but she only curled a tiny hand around the swell of my breast and sucked happily. Smith strode into the room and stopped short when he saw us like this. I braced for a lecture about being alone with the baby. Instead, his rigid shoulders relaxed.

"How is Nora?" I asked.

"She's going to be fine. The paramedics said she needs to get an EpiPen to keep up with her. Apparently she's never had a reaction this bad before." He took a hesitant step forward, his eyes raking over the two of us. "How are you?"

Part of me didn't want to jinx it, so I simply shrugged. "I don't know if she's getting anything or not."

"She doesn't seem angry. That seems like a good sign."

I thought so, too. Maybe she'd had a recent bottle and didn't need my milk as much. Regardless, it felt right to have her in my arms.

"What is Nora allergic to?" I asked absently.

"Nuts," he said in a measured tone. "Did you know she had an allergy?"

I searched my brain for any memory of her telling me. Finally, I shook my head. "No. She probably should've told us."

"Mrs. Winters is on a tear," he warned me. "I think she feels responsible. She gave her a Christmas cake with walnuts in it. Nora didn't realize."

"You think she'd be more careful," I said wondering how Nora could let something like that go without mentioning.

"That's just it." Smith paced over to the fireplace to stoke the logs. A blast of sparks shot up from the wood and the fire roared more strongly. "She said she mentioned it to you. Apparently, it was also on her application."

I stared at his profile, wishing I could see his face fully. The fire cast shadows on it now that made me shiver. "I don't remember seeing that at all."

"You have a lot going on. Now we know, and nothing terrible happened."

He was handling me again. Nora had told me, and I'd forgotten to warn Mrs. Winters. Both would trust me a little less now, and I'd have very little of their trust to begin with.

"Are you sure about that?" I asked softly, guilt taking hold of me again. "Because if medical help was sent for—"

"Don't blame yourself for this. I'm just as responsible for not knowing as you," he pointed out. "Like you said, now we know."

I bobbed my head, trying to believe him. He made a good argument. Then again, he was a lawyer. Still, I couldn't shake the feeling of once more failing in my responsibilities. I left Nora with my baby, trusting her to be able to care for my helpless infant and yet, I hadn't done enough to protect the nanny.

"I'm going through all the employee files tomorrow," I decided. "I won't let this happen again." It was one thing to be sorry, it was another thing to do something about it.

"I don't think that's necessary," Smith said so swiftly that I raised an eyebrow. "I just mean that I can do that. You have your hands full."

"Alright," I agreed. I hesitated a moment, before adding, "Smith, stay close by tonight." I wanted to believe that I had all of this under control, but I wouldn't risk Penny's welfare again. I had to put her needs above my pride.

"Wild horses," he said, signaling that he understood. He sank into the other chair, and I looked over at him. He ditched his suit jacket somewhere along with his tie. As he settled, he reached up and unfastened his top button. His cufflinks followed. He was tired, but his evening stubble had grown darker, and I found myself thinking of how good it felt when it scratched along my inner thigh. He tossed the cufflinks on the chair side table, watching me with a burning intensity that reminded me that less than an hour ago we'd been pulled over on the snowy side of the road, promising each other forever the best way we knew how. A crooked smile hooked his mouth as if he was thinking the same thing, and, for just a moment, we were the couple cut from the catalog. Wife and husband, mother, father, and the precious gifts our love had given us. We had the world in this room. For just a moment, everything was perfect.

"Why don't you take a break?" Smith asked, leaning down to take Penny from me. She'd been sleeping peacefully for the last hour, and I wasn't certain I wanted to give her up just yet. I wanted to soak up these peaceful moments with her before returning to the chaos of the real world. That said, I needed a glass of water and a trip to the loo. Plus, there was nothing sexier than seeing Smith with Penny.

She started a little as he lifted her into his arm, and he hushed her softly, rocking her back and forth as I rose from the glider and stretched. He took the seat I'd vacated, his eyes never leaving his sleeping bundle. There was none of the cocky arrogance I'd first fallen in love with when he held her, there was only a hushed reverence bordering on worshipfulness that made me fall in love with him all over again.

The rest of the house was quiet when I headed toward the kitchen. Edward hadn't come in from the party as far as I knew. I was going to have to ask him how things went with Tomas in the morning. Given that I'd left him with Jane, there was no telling how much trouble he'd gotten into. I flipped on the kitchen lights and turned, nearly jumping out of my skin when I found Mrs. Winters sitting at the table.

"You scared me," I said. Had she been sitting alone in the dark? I studied her for a moment. Her eyes were red-rimmed and she was clutching a mug tightly in her white-knuckled grip.

"Seems fair, given how much your oversight scared me," she said in a cold voice.

"I didn't know that Nora..." I trailed away, torn between feeling surprised by her reaction and feeling guilty because I knew she was somewhat right.

"Can I get you something, ma'am?" she asked dutifully, pushing her chair back. Its legs scraped across the floor more loudly in the sleeping house.

"I'm just getting a glass of water," I said, heading over to the cabinets. I took a glass down and filled it. Drinking it in silence, I considered how to make this right for her.

"I must have overlooked the information in her application," I said for Mrs. Winters's benefit. "There was so much happening with the remodel and the baby. Smith and I are going to go through all of the employee files and make sure nothing like this ever happens again."

"Yes, ma'am." She bobbed her head at me before rising slowly, wobbling a little on her feet.

"Are you feeling well?" I asked in concern as she swayed on her feet.

"I'm just fine," she snapped. "I'll be going down to bed unless you need me."

I shook my head. Mrs. Winters disappeared down the narrow servant's staircase toward her quarters on the ground floor.. I waited until she was gone and walked over to the table. Picking up the mug she was drinking from, I sniffed it and immediately gasped as the sting of whiskey hit my nostrils. No wonder she'd been shaky on her feet. It wasn't my place to judge a grown woman's drinking choices, especially on New Year's Eve, but I couldn't help wondering if Mrs. Winters was a mean drunk, given how rudely she'd just spoken to me.

I carried the cup to the sink and rinsed it out, leaving it on the counter. Tonight had been too much for all of us. We had all been through a lot lately. But it was a new year, and I was determined that in the morning we would turn over a new leaf accordingly. I opened the rubbish bin to dump my tea leaves and saw the crumpled remains of the fruitcake there. No doubt it was the one that had caused Nora's allergic reaction.

Making my way upstairs, I paused at her room and knocked softly before peeking in. "I just wanted to check on you. I hope you weren't sleeping."

"I think I'm a bit too shaken up to sleep," she admitted, biting her lip. "I'm sorry to ruin your night."

"Don't apologize to me," I said firmly. "I should have known about your allergy."

"I thought you did," she said with some hesitation. "It was on my application, and I brought it up to you personally."

"Honestly, I've had baby brain for a while." It was the nicest way to say that I hadn't had my shit together of late.

"I'm not upset with you," she said quickly. "I didn't mean to suggest that."

"I barely remember anything before Penny was born. Everything was happening all at once."

"Oh no, Belle, it was after I came to help you with Penny." She cocked her head at my puzzled face. "You don't remember? You said you would tell Mrs. Winters. It's why I didn't worry about the fruitcake. Normally, I avoid them."

"It must've slipped my mind." It was a lie. I had no recollection of her mentioning it, but those had been sleep deprived days. "Is there anything I can get you?"

"I'm fine. I promise I'll be back up to help you with the baby in the morning. I'm supposed to rest for now."

"Take all the time you need. Smith and I are taking turns with Penny.

"I just don't want you to think I'm not available," she said meaningfully.

I forced a smile, I didn't need another reminder that she'd taken over the task of being Penny's primary caregiver. "We'll be fine. I'm glad that you're okay. Good night."

She settled against her pillow and smiled. "Good night."

I closed the door behind me and started toward the nursery. I paused as I reached Smith's study. I wanted to see Nora's application for myself. This shouldn't have happened.. I went to his desk, prepared to rifle through his drawers to look for the employee files but found a stack of them on top of his desk instead. I sorted through them, looking for Nora's but hers was the only one not on the desk. Naturally.

I opened his file drawer and thumbed through the hanging folders. There was paperwork regarding Thornham. The lease to his offices that he'd completely ignored since Penny's arrival. Information pertinent to my own business. Our will. But Nora's file was nowhere to be found. I looked through the stack on his desk again. All I had wanted was to see it there in black and white, and prove to myself that was an innocent oversight. But as I returned the files to the stack, I couldn't help wondering where Nora's information was—and who had it.

SMITH

Breakfast the next morning was a somber affair. Mrs. Winters seemed to be suffering from a headache and delivered plates to the table like she was doling out punishments. I said nothing as I took a seat, Penny in my arms. Belle had stayed up with her most of the night and was having a well deserved late start.

"Morning." Georgia looked fresher than the rest of us as she came in through the back door. She had disappeared to the guesthouse almost as soon as we returned from the party. I still haven't seen Edward or Jane. I wasn't certain either had come last night.

"Sleep well?" I asked dryly.

She pulled out the chair next to me, it screeched on the stone floor and Penny stirred restlessly in my arms.

"Great. My housemate didn't come home." She cut a bit of sausage with the edge of her fork and shoveled into her mouth.

"Jane had her eye on a gentleman at the party," I told her.

"I think she caught him." Georgia continued to eat like everything was normal. I stole a glance at Mrs. Winters and caught her glaring at us. She turned around swiftly and busied herself putting a kettle on.

"Should I save a plate for the missus?" she called over her shoulder. "Or take up some tea?"

"She was up with the baby most of the night," I said. "I think we should let her rest."

Mrs. Winters turned off the hob and huffed out of the room towards the pantry.

"She's in a good mood," Georgia muttered.

"Belle said she reprimanded her last night. She seems to think it's Belle's fault that Nora ate those nuts.

"That is actually nuts," Georgia said emphatically. "No pun intended. It's not like she shoved them down her throat."

"I said the same thing. But it seemed as though Mrs. Winters is holding a grudge."

"I was thinking—" Georgia cut off as Nora entered the kitchen.

It was hard to believe that she'd needed medical help last night. She waltzed into the room, smiling from ear to ear and came straight over. "I can take the baby now."

"You should have some breakfast," I said. "After what you went through last night. You must be hungry."

"You're so sweet," she said appreciatively. "I came down earlier and made myself some toast. I guess I was up before everyone else."

That must be another reason that Mrs. Winters was unhappy. She prided herself on feeding everyone and didn't appreciate it when someone beat her to the task. I passed Penny to Nora, who kissed her head affectionately.

"I missed you, Penny girl." She carried the baby off in the direction of the nursery, and I tucked into my breakfast properly.

I had a mouthful of sausage when I remembered Georgia had been mid sentence when Nora walked in. I swallowed the bite hard, but before I could prompt her, Georgia put down her fork and gave me a serious look.

"Price, be careful there."

"Nora?" I said, wanting to laugh. "I'm not remotely—"

"You're not the one I'm worried about."

I frowned. "What does that mean?"

"You're so sweet," she imitated Nora, batting her lashes for effect.

"She's a kid." I returned to my breakfast. The nanny was the least of our worries.

"My point exactly." She heaved a uniquely feminine sigh of disapproval before getting back to business. "I think we should talk to Roman."

"I thought you weren't worried about him."

"I'm not. He doesn't strike me as someone to worry about, but he was here when the Thornes lived on the property. That means he knows better than anyone what might've been going on in this house before the disappearances."

She was probably right about that, but Rowan might

not cooperate. He was grumpy on his best days. I couldn't imagine he'd appreciate an interrogation.

I speared another bite of sausage. "After breakfast."

We found Rowan near the stables, tending to the landscaping he'd installed around the Bless offices. The snow was wreaking havoc on a number of the rose bushes he'd been caring for through the fall. As we approached, I caught a string of muttered curses as he scooped mounds of snow away from the flowers.

"See why we're not worried," I said under my breath.

"He still might know something."

As we approached, Rowan whipped around, taking a defensive posture like he'd been cornered. He relaxed when he saw my face. "Oh, it's you."

It was a good thing the man worked with plants more than people. "How's it coming?"

Georgia shot me a look that said she didn't approve buttering him up, but didn't speak.

Judging by the look on Rowan's weathered face, he didn't approve of small talk either.

"Fine. Wish this bloody snow would stop." He shook a bit more snow off his precious plants and continued, "Heard there was a bit of excitement here last night."

Rowan, unlike the rest of the staff, didn't live on the estate. He had a home in the village. I had no idea why, given that he seemed to be here during every daylight hour and then some. He was always on property before I'd risen for the day and never left before supper.

"Yes. An accident," I told him.

"Thornham's always had more than its fair share of accidents," he said darkly.

"Actually," Georgia jumped in, seizing her window of opportunity as soon as he spoke. "That's what we want to talk to you about."

"About what?" He raised one bushy eyebrow, pausing to reach for a shovel before starting to clear the path leading to the offices.

"That's not necessary," I said. "I doubt Belle will make it into the office today."

"It's better to do it now than let more collect," he said stubbornly and continued his work.

"We wanted to ask you about your old job," Georgia said, shifting the conversation back to what we had come to discuss. "More specifically about when you worked here before."

"It was nearly fifty years ago." He paused and rested the shovel in the snow. "And I didn't work here for long."

"We were just curious. We've heard some stories in the village," I said. I didn't want to press the old man. If he was unwilling to share, so be it.

"I was only eighteen. They kept a full staff of gardeners," he explained. "Like I said, I wasn't here that long."

"Okay, then, "Georgia said in a disappointed tone.

"But my older brother had been working here for five years before the disappearances," Rowan went on. He went back to shoveling and continued, "The stories he told. Like I said, lots of accidents."

"What kind of accidents?" I asked. Maybe it was the

cold air around me or the snow, but my body seemed to be kicking into some type of survival mode. Blood roared in my ears. Why hadn't we learned about Thornham's past before we purchased the place? Why did I think it mattered now?

"Little ones, most of them," Rowan said as though this explained it. "One child would push another. A broken arm. Then there was the incident on the roof."

"The roof?" Georgia repeated.

"Some say one of the girls slipped," he said. "Others say she jumped. She claims she was pushed."

"She fell off the roof?" I asked, my gaze traveling instinctively to look at the house. Even at this distance, it loomed along the horizon. I couldn't imagine anyone surviving that fall, especially with the driveway below.

"Not that roof," he said. He pointed the shovel at the former stables. "That roof."

"Was she okay?" Georgia asked.

"She hit her head. Some say she forgot things after that. I suppose it hardly matters. She's gone now."

"Do you know where they went?" Georgia asked innocently.

A muscle in his jaw ticked as he shrugged. "I suppose that's what they found in your basement. Everyone always suspected they were dead. They think it was the mother that did it."

"Her bones weren't down there," I confirmed. "And I know people around the village claim to have seen her over the years."

"That's rubbish." Rowan laughed and resumed shoveling.

His reaction struck me as odd. He clearly put some stock in the rumors about the Thorne family."Why's that?"

"Because they couldn't have seen her. But that won't stop the village from talking. Nobody has anything better to do than imagine wild stories."

"How do you know?" I asked carefully.

He stopped and looked me in the eye. "Because Miranda Thorne is in an insane asylum in Brighton."

I WAS STILL PROCESSING ROWAN'S REVELATION WHEN I reached the house, realizing we had new company. I tore inside the house. Racing upstairs, I found the doctor leaving my bedroom. He stepped through the door and shut it with a gentle smile.

"Is everything okay?" I asked.

"I was just here checking on Mrs. Price. I'm sorry it took me so long to get by. With the holidays I'm stretched a little thin."

I found myself making a mental note to make a financial contribution to the local clinic that would ensure we found ourselves on the top of his list in the future.

He looked at me for a moment, then turned and made sure the bedroom door was completely closed behind him. Lowering his voice, he said, "Can you tell me about what happened the other day? Mrs. Price's recollection of the event seems to be a little fuzzy."

I filled the doctor in on what I remembered from that day, everything from the milk supply all the way to finding her on the ice, and how concerned she'd been to be with Penny alone after that. He listened without comment until I stopped.

Then he nodded his head thoughtfully. "Mrs. Price seems concerned that it's down to her antidepressant, but it shouldn't be causing that. It is possible that it's a side effect of the sleeping tablets I gave her, but she claims she's not taking them very often."

"I think she took one that morning." She'd been in a state after Penny had been inconsolable. I hadn't thought anything of it.

"Then it's best for her to avoid them. Some people are known to sleepwalk while taking them. It's very rare," he added quickly when he saw my face. "Although, I did have a patient drive all the way to Surrey without realizing it once."

I stared at him, wondering if he had earned his medical degree online, but kept the thought to myself. "We'll definitely avoid it. Is there anything she can take to help her sleep?"

"Best stick to an herbal tea. I'm sure she'll recognize a camomile properly," he said with a wink.

"I'm sure she will, too," I said, not hiding a caustic note in my voice. I was beginning to rethink my donation to the local clinic. Maybe it was best if I took Belle to see a doctor in London in the future. She certainly didn't need an old wanker condescending to her.

"I left a week's supply of her new medication for her,"

he told me, missing my anger entirely. "You'll need to have the rest picked up at the pharmacy."

I nodded, moving closer to the door. I wanted to check on her and see if the good doctor had irritated her as much as he did me.

"Mr. Price," he said, stopping at the top of the staircase. "Detective Longborn mentioned you were looking into the Thornes."

My hand froze on the nob, and I nodded.

"I treated Mrs. Thorne, too. Small village."

"Was what they say about her true?" I asked.

"Some called her crazy," he said, saying what I hadn't. "I don't like to use that term, but that's as close as I've ever come to true insanity."

I studied him for a moment, an icy hand wrapping itself around my heart as I considered what he was really saying. "Why are you telling me this?"

"Because I had the chance fifty years ago to intervene," he said sadly, "but I was young and foolish, so I didn't. The accidents. The stories we heard. Someone should have done something then. Just like someone has to do something now."

"What are you saying?" I asked. I wanted to hear him say it.

"I'd keep a careful eye on your wife, Mr. Price. Thornham does funny things to people." He tipped his hat and continued down the stairs, leaving me with more questions than answers.

Jane passed him on the stairs. It was the first time I'd seen her since the party last night. She smiled warmly at the doctor before floating the rest of the way up. "I came to check on her. Edward filled me in on what happened last night. It sounds like a tragic accident to me."

"It was, but Belle blames herself." I managed to force the corners of my lips up a little.

"She's always been the motherly type," Jane said with a sigh. "I saw it when she lived with Clara, and, of course, she had to take care of herself when she was a child. She's too hard on herself for her own good." Jane's eyes narrowed into a shrewd look. "That's why you must go easy on her."

"I try," I promised. But I couldn't help feeling as though I was failing. If Jane was right, what Belle needed most was someone to take care of her. "I feel like she doesn't want me to mother her."

Jane laughed, shaking her platinum head. "Don't mother her! I'm afraid you've misunderstood me. Just be her refuge. That's all any of us want from love: a safe place in someone's arms."

"Is she giving you advice?" Belle asked, startling us both. "She's always giving relationship advice."

"That's because I know what I'm talking about," Jane said, recovering quickly. She moved to Belle's side and tucked a loose strand of hair behind her ears. "Do you want to tell me about your night—or should I tell you about mine?"

Belle laughed for the first time all day. "I think I'd rather hear about your night."

"Hughes has already asked me to go to Paris," Jane told her, steering her back towards the bedroom. She tossed me a wink before she closed the door to gossip. It was a good distraction for Belle—for the moment. But if I knew Jane, she'd depart in the same flurry of activity she arrived in.

I found myself walking down the hall, not really clear on where I was going. Somehow, I found myself at Edward's door. I knocked, wondering if he'd made it back yet either. He opened the door, sporting bed-head. He squinted at the light in the hall and held a hand up to block it from his face.

"Hungover?"

"More than a little." He closed both eyes as if words actually hurt to speak. "Need something?"

"I was thinking that maybe Belle could use some time away from the house."

Edward drew a breath, and I knew he understood why I was bringing this up. "She wanted to go to London for a shopping trip."

"I'll talk to Georgia."

"I don't know if we need—"

I flashed him a don't-fuck-with-me look and he shut his mouth. "I'll talk to Belle."

12

BELLE

"If you check your phone one more time, I'm going to confiscate it." Edward had taken the backseat, which had only left him craning to see what I was doing in the front. He leaned over my shoulder and swatted my arm. "We've only been gone an hour."

"I know." I turned off my screen and placed my mobile in my lap, already feeling the urge to check one more time.

"Give her a break," Georgia said from the driver's seat. "This is the first time you've been this far away from Penny, isn't it?"

I swallowed and nodded. The last few days had been calm at Thornham since Nora's accident on New Year's Eve. But calm at Thornham felt like a relative concept. I hadn't wanted to leave the estate. Edward had insisted we go through with taking our shopping trip to London. Jane had left the day before, swept off to Paris by Hughes, and I wasn't entirely certain when she might return. That made finishing her guest room feel less important. I doubted

Georgia cared very much about her living space. But Edward's insistence was both infectious and persuasive. I got the impression he needed a shopping trip more than I did. I'd finally agreed, and then, Smith had insisted that Georgia drive us. I'd wanted to take Penny along, but I was met with resistance on all sides. It seemed I "deserved a break from the baby." I couldn't help thinking that it had less to do with a break and more to do with no one trusting me to handle her for a whole day in the city. I'd lost the debate, and now Penny was home with Nora. I had even managed to pump a few bottles of breast milk so she wouldn't have to give Penny formula. She was in good hands. Smith would be there the whole time. Still, I found myself nervously tapping the sleek black console of Georgia's Porsche.

"Maybe we need to get her drunk," Edward piped up helpfully.

"I really am going to have to babysit you two," Georgia muttered, exiting the M25. Spotting a sign for Heathrow, my nerves shifted. Despite my worry about leaving Penny behind, my excitement grew with each mile that took us closer to the city. I hadn't been back since Penny was born, and I had spent most of that trip trying to go into labor. This would be the first time in months that I could walk around freely, doing whatever I wanted. I didn't care what Georgia thought, this called for champagne.

When we reached Harrods, Georgia pulled directly up to the entrance. She ignored the door attendant clad in his pea green uniform, trying to wave her down. "I'll be in in a few minutes. Behave yourself."

"Yes, mum," Edward teased her as we made our way out.

"I'm sorry but there's no parking—" The man immediately froze when he spotted Edward and moved to the door. People in the crowd, who'd turned to look at the renegade Porsche, began to whisper. For one second, the paranoia I'd felt since moving to Thornham took hold, and I gripped Edward's arm. He dragged me inside with practiced disinterest, nodding to a security guard, who moved to block the curious onlookers from following us.

"I haven't missed that," he gritted out.

"Honestly, I forgot how much of a stir you cause."

"Trust me, it's been worse the last few months." He forced a smile, but it was flat on the edges like his body wanted to grimace instead.

I could only imagine after his husband died so soon after their overly politicized marriage that the reporters had been relentless. The last time we'd been here before Penny was born, he'd kept a low profile by sporting a style that was somewhere between panhandler and rockstar chic. Now, in his pressed khaki trousers and oxford button-down, he was instantly recognizable.

"Where to first?" he asked, displaying a remarkable tenacity for forgetting that dozens of people had just stopped to gawk at him. The looks continued inside, but due to the upscale nature of Harrods where it wasn't unusual to see a celebrity, or in this case a prince, shopping amongst you, no one approached us.

"Third floor," I chirped. We were here for the guesthouse, not ourselves, which meant going to the home department.

"Okay, but I have strict instructions from Smith," he confessed to me.

My eyes shuttered for a moment, wondering if I'd even be allowed to use the loo alone, but to my surprise, Edward added, "He says I'm to make sure you pick up something really expensive, and really useless, for yourself."

"Am I, now?" I said with a laugh. I shouldn't be surprised. Smith had always known how to spoil a girl. I'd once discovered he bought the entire fall collection of Louboutins and had it delivered to his closet for my use.

"Deal." I dragged him toward the lifts, bypassing the bronze escalators that led to more tempting pursuits. It also avoided a half dozen new arrivals who were pointing at Edward like they were visiting a zoo. "But first, let's figure out what to do about the guesthouse."

Part of me had hoped that Georgia would take the opportunity to return to London full time on this trip, but she'd insisted on driving us here *and* back. Whatever she was up to with Smith, they were still in the thick of it. I chose to trust my husband, not pushing him for answers as to the real reason behind her stay. I knew he wanted to keep an extra set of eyes on me and the baby, but it was more than that. Doubt tickled the back of my mind. We'd been through this before, but then he'd been more honest about what was happening. I didn't know if he was trying to keep me from more anxiety or if he saw *me* as the primary danger confronting us.

"Don't do that," Edward said, breaking into my

thoughts as the lift dinged, announcing we'd reached the third floor.

"What?" I asked, blinking and trying to get my attention back on him.

"You're worrying," he told me. "I'm going to have to start plying you with champagne before noon if you don't stop."

"I'm not sure Smith would approve of that." I trailed my finger along a table, displaying a lovely selection of Wedgwood plates as we made our way to the bath and bed linens.

"It was his idea."

"It was?" I stopped.

"Well," Edward hedged, nudging me onward, "he said to make sure you enjoyed yourself by any means necessary."

"That sounds like permission to me." I couldn't help giggling as I looped my arm through my best friend's. All around us, displays of luxury fabrics and bespoke decor tempted shoppers into redoing every room in their house. Thankfully, most of Thornham had been recently decorated or I might find myself spending a small fortune. Shop attendants murmured hello's and polite questions as we passed, but we simply nodded and thanked them. The one nice thing about the luxury store was how well it trained it's employees to be helpful but not bothersome. Still, we were gathering the usual amount of interest I expected anywhere I went with Edward.

"What about this one?" He asked, pointing to a classic Ralph Lauren-designed bedding set, its tartan duvet cover perfectly complimenting a thick, navy velvet coverlet. It was simple, elegant, and would do for most guests. I nodded. "That will be good for Georgia's room."

"But I suppose we should do something a little more eccentric for Jane?" he guessed.

"Other people will stay there," I murmured, considering my options, "but I want Jane to visit as often as possible and feel comfortable." We meandered over to a different display, this one with silk sheets in rich, jewel tones. I was debating whether I should continue the blue into the other side of the guest house or go with the deep plum color I preferred when Edward muttered beside me," Are you fucking kidding me?"

"What?" I looked up to see Georgia striding toward us, but she wasn't alone. My eyes flashed to Edward, worried that he might explode or make a run for it, but all he did was stand there with clenched fists as Clara made her way to us, pushing a pram.

She shot me a nervous smile. If there had been attention on us before, it would be unbearable soon. I looked around, prepared to step between Clara and other shopper's mobile phone cameras, but the department was curiously empty save for the sales associates. We'd been duped. Georgia told Clara we would be here, and Clara had arranged to crash our shopping date.

"I hope you don't mind if I join you," Clara called, maintaining a safe distance by staying behind the pram. Her eyes flickered to Edward before skittering quickly back to me.

"We're just surprised," I said quickly. I circled around

the baby carriage and gave her a tight hug. Lowering my voice, I whispered, "I don't know how he's going to react to this."

"I know," she whispered back. "But since neither of you return my calls I didn't have any other choice."

Loneliness trembled in her voice. Clara was happy in her marriage to Alexander. The two adored each other with an obsession that dictated their every move. But he was a powerful man, and with that power came responsibilities that meant they couldn't be together all the time. I thought of how it felt to be cooped up in Thornham for the last few months and sympathy swelled inside me. How much worse had it been for Clara during that time? She couldn't go anywhere without a security entourage. After her kidnapping, Alexander and her rarely left Buckingham. And the whole time she's been doing that without a word from her best friends. Edward had every right to maintain his distance after what had happened, but what excuse did I have? I'd even unintentionally claimed her only companion, drawing Georgia to Briarshead to help me and Smith.

"Sorry," I said earnestly. "I've been a cunt."

"You have a baby," she said with a laugh at my choice of words. "But I did hear some things that worried me."

"Later," I promised her. The truth was that talking to Clara might help me understand more of what was going on in my head. Clara had been through pregnancy. Clara had faced uncertainty and danger. She had children of her own. Suddenly, I couldn't remember why I had been avoiding her in the first place. It was strange how much clearer everything seemed in London compared to Thornham. Problems didn't seem as insurmountable here.

We broke apart. Clara looked over my shoulder apprehensively. She waited for a moment for Edward to speak. When he didn't, I turned, sliding my arm around Clara's waist, and gave him a barbed look. I understood the gamut of emotions he felt when he saw her. We'd discussed the confusion that came as a result of David's death and Clara's disappearance before.

Clara swayed on her feet a little, her free hand wrapped tightly around the handle of the baby carriage. I nudged her forward with my palm. "You two should talk."

I moved over and took the pram from her, strolling with it towards the display I'd been looking at a moment ago. Leaning down, I lifted Wills, who gurgled with pleasure at the sight of my face.

"Remember me?" I asked him softly.

He grinned more widely. Seeing him, I remembered all the time I had spent at Buckingham leading up to Penny's birth. Helping with Wills had felt natural. Why had it been so hard with Penny? I knew that my hormones changed and that it was a different kind of responsibility, but putting Wills on my hip while he reached for my necklace, I was left to wonder if maybe I was better with babies than I thought. Why could I only see this here? Why had we decided to move to the country?

I forced myself to return to my perusal of the bedding for Jane's guest room, stealing glances at Edward and Clara as I did. Georgia joined me and pretended to be interested in shopping.

"How's it going?" I asked in a low voice.

"No one's dead yet." She picked up a pillow sham, turned it over like she never seen it one before, and put it back down.

"You could have warned me," I told her.

"I wasn't giving either of you the chance to back out of this. Honestly, the holidays were very hard on Clara. She's had a lot of nightmares. Alexander makes her feel better, but sometimes a girl needs her best friends." It was an oddly thoughtful move on Georgia's part, I realized. I knew she'd grown closer to Clara, but it occurred to me that Georgia might not be as cold as I thought.

I swallowed against the guilt that rose inside me as I heard this. I'd been so consumed with my own concerns that I'd never stopped to wonder if Clara was calling because she needed me.

"I wish we had never left London," I said, surprising myself.

Georgia snorted, her attention devoted to analyzing throw pillows. "Out with it. If you have an opinion, share it."

"Smith thought he could run from trouble, but I don't know why he can't see—"

"That trouble always finds us?" I finished for her. I sighed, deciding on the plum color. Not everything in life had to match perfectly. Not everything in life could. Thornham proved just that. "I don't want to stay there anymore."

"I know," Georgia said simply. "I'm working on it."

I wanted to ask her what she meant by that, but we

were interrupted by Clara and Edward Both of them had tears in their eyes as they joined us. Edward hesitated a moment before holding out his arms for Wills.

"Do you mind if I hold my nephew?"

I glanced at Clara, realizing her tears were happy ones. It was a good reminder that tears come as often with joy as sadness. "Not at all."

Georgia was right. We wouldn't solve anything by hiding from our problems, especially if our problems were going to follow us. We had to face them. I just had to get Smith to see that London was the place to make our stand.

13

SMITH

If Belle thought that Penny wouldn't miss her, she was wrong. Nora and I had been taking turns for the last few hours passing the baby back and forth, but Penny remained inconsolable. She wanted her mother, and no one else would do. Still, I was grateful the young nanny was here to help me. Especially after circling the nursery for the last hour until Penny tired herself out.

I walked into the kitchen triumphantly, carrying a sleeping baby to find Mrs. Winters digging into the pantry.

"Is everything okay?" I asked in a low voice, not wanting to wake Penny up.

Mrs. Winters turned, a startled hand flying to her cheek, her eyes in a daze. She shook her head as if to clear it. "Quite."

The housekeeper had been acting strangely since Nora's allergic reaction. She blamed herself, which for the old battle ax meant projecting that guilt on everyone around her. I took a step forward and examined the array of items on the counter.

"Clearing out the cupboards?"

Her face pinched into a look that would have withered fruit on the spot. It merely amused me. "If you must know, I'm getting rid of allergens."

"I think nuts are the only thing you need to worry about," I said.

That was a mistake. She whipped around, planting her hands on her ample hips and leveled the full-force of her glare at me. "How do we know that? What if the baby has an allergy? What if—"

"No one blames you," I interrupted her. In all of the confusion on New Year's, I'm not sure anyone had told her that. I'd been concerned about Belle. Belle had been concerned about Nora. Georgia...

Well, it was hard to say who Georgia was concerned about at any given time.

Mrs. Winters returned to her work, but her shoulders trembled a little. A moment later, she turned with the box in her hands and a puzzled look on her face. "Why was that back here?" She placed it on the counter and then turned to another cupboard. She pulled out a tea tin. Prying off the lid, she sniffed and her puzzled gaze returned to the box.

"What is it?"

"I think it's some of that lactation tea Mrs. Price was told to drink."

"What's she been drinking?" I couldn't bear a repeat of what happened the morning Belle's milk supply had failed her. I wasn't sure she would recover from that a second time.

"That's just it. She hasn't been drinking the tea. She doesn't like the taste of it. It was easier to get her to drink the other. That means this—" she rattled the tin "—is nearly full."

"I only brought home one box," I said slowly.

"This must be the one she brought home the first time, but then..." She stared at it for a moment longer, shrugged her shoulders, and moved it to the cupboard where she kept the tea.

There was only one explanation for how that box got into the house. Belle had brought it home. If that was the case, how had she wound up with the wrong one? I might cross it off as an innocent mistake if the tea she'd been drinking hadn't caused the exact problem she was hoping to avoid. I wished she was here now, so she could see it. But she was in London, and I didn't want to disturb her. Georgia had been checking in with me, sending me quick text messages to let me know the shopping trip was going well, but, more than ever, I found myself wishing I was there with Belle. Before I could fully process what this meant, my mobile began to ring.

"Excuse me." I carried Penny out of the kitchen, shifting her to my shoulder to answer it. "Hello?"

"Hello, Mr. Price," the booming voice of our estate agent, Dennis, greeted me. "I confess I hadn't expected to hear from you so soon? You're not sick of Thornham, already?" He laughed at his own joke.

I grimaced. If he knew what was going on here, he

wouldn't think it a laughing matter. "Actually, I had a question. I was recently told the estate wasn't for sale when we viewed it. Is that true?"

There was a pause and I could almost see him shifting from his laid back position, feet up on his desk and mobile at his ear, to sit upright. "Well, no. It wasn't. That's not odd, though," he added swiftly. "These old family homes rarely get placed on the market. Most buyers and sellers handle things privately."

"But the family was gone," I pointed out, shifting on my feet as Penny stirred in my arms. "Why wouldn't it have been put on the market?"

"I...don't know," he admitted. "I can look into the matter more if there is a concern, but I assure your purchase was completely legal."

I imagined this conversation had sent a cold sweat forming on his brow. He thought he was simply calling a prior client. He hadn't expected an interrogation. Maybe if he had, he would have been more helpful.

"That won't be necessary," I reassured him. "I only wanted to check."

"Of course." There was a rush of air like he'd exhaled in relief. "Is there anything else I can help you with? I know we discussed the possibility of placing your London home—"

"Not at the moment. Actually," I paused and reconsidered. "How did you hear about Thornham if it wasn't for sale?"

"We get tips all the time. Probably a local let us know.

Some village busybody who was tired of seeing the place fall to ruin."

"That makes sense," I said tightly. I thanked him for his time and hung up. I hadn't learned much—nothing concrete, at least—but he had confirmed what Georgia had told me.

The estate hadn't been for sale. Months ago, I might have accepted his explanation for how we wound up learning about it. Now?

None of this added up. Everything Georgia had uncovered thus far had been confirmed by police reports and county records. The family had disappeared, only to have us unearth their remains decades later. And according to Rowan, the rumors of the village were true. Miranda Thorne was alive. Was it possible that there was no ghostly specter of our past causing this problem, instead had we wandered into someone else's tragedy and accidentally filled the vacancies the Thorne family's deaths had left behind?

Nora came bouncing down the stairs and saw me struggling to send a text.

"Let me have her." She picked up the baby. "I honestly can do this myself."

I'd been arguing with her about that all day. Now I was grateful for the reprieve.

"Would you mind if I looked into a few things?" I asked her, relieved there was someone to rely on here.

"I'm always here for you, Smith." She turned on her heel and carried Penny carefully upstairs toward the nursery.

I'd gotten to the second line of my text to Georgia when it occurred to me that Nora had never called me by my first name before. I suppose it made sense, given that she was here full-time Belle insisted on being called by her first name. Still, it didn't sit well with me. Then again nothing seemed quite right in Briarshead these days. I thought we'd left London behind for a simpler life, but now I had to face facts. Nothing was ever simple where we were concerned.

14

BELLE

It was official. Edward was a natural with babies. I'd seen him enough with Penny to know that he felt fairly comfortable around them, but watching him with Wills, who was a few months older, proved to me that not only was he an excellent uncle, someday he would be an amazing father. If he ever found love again.

"He adores you," I said as Edward and Wills played pat-a-cake on the ground. Harrods had kindly cleared The Penthouse, their private shopping space, for us to have afternoon tea. They probably wanted to avoid the spectacle that trying to dine with half the royal family would cause as much as we did. This seemed to relieve Georgia, who'd busied herself on her phone for the better part of the afternoon once we'd been locked away somewhere safe. Clara lounged comfortably next to me on a gray suede couch and sighed happily as we watched her brother-in-law play with her son.

"Maybe you'll start coming around more," she said hopefully.

Edward's answering smile was tight. "I'm planning on going back to the country with Belle."

"You can't possibly want to go back to Briarshead," I said.

An eyebrow quirked over the rim of his glasses. "Ready to get rid of me?"

"Never," I promised. It wasn't that I wanted my best friend to leave Thornham. It was that I wanted to stay in London. "But you're going to be bored. I have to get into my new offices tomorrow and deal with some Bless orders for the new season."

"I can manage myself. It turns out there's some fun things to do in the country." This time his grin was more genuine.

"That reminds me," I said, snapping my fingers. "When did you come home on New Year's Eve?"

"No one is supposed to come home on New Year's Eve," he told me seriously. "I was out past midnight."

"Careful," Clara interjected, "or you'll turn into a pumpkin."

"The prince isn't the one who turns into a pumpkin," he said dryly.

"He's the one chasing after the girl he met at the party," I confirmed, siding with him. "Sounds more like you and Alexander."

Silence fell immediately, and I realized what I'd done wrong. We'd managed to keep his name out of conversation thus far, allowing Edward and Clara space to work towards rebuilding their relationship. Reminding Edward of his brother wasn't going to help with that.

"So, what is there to do in Briarshead?" Clara said quickly, steering the conversation back to less dangerous waters.

"Not what," I told her, "but *who*."

"Oh really?" She clapped her hands excitedly. "I want to hear about it."

"There's nothing to tell." Edward turned the page of a board book for Wills. "I made a friend."

"Who he stayed out with well past midnight," I added with emphasis.

"Would this be a single, male friend?" Clara asked.

"This would be a single, hot, *French chef* male friend," I said. Even to me that sounded promising.

"We were just having fun," Edward said flatly, refusing to meet our eyes. Clara and I looked at each other. Apparently we were a way off from matchmaking with him.

"Did you find everything you need?" Clara asked, changing the subject again. Apparently, we were going to stick to the safest conversation of all: shopping.

"I think so." I listed out the items I'd already purchased in my head. "Honestly, I just want them to feel a little more comfortable. Not that Georgia minds, but I want Jane to feel at home the next time she visits."

"You've had a lot of visitors considering you have a newborn."

"Yeah, we needed some help with Penny," I admitted sheepishly.

Edward had carried Wills to the window to show him

the cars moving along the street below, so I took my opportunity to speak to Clara privately. "Did you ever have postpartum depression?"

Clara's face softened instantly, and she reached out her hand, placing it on mine. "A little. It hasn't been too bad for me."

"Oh." I suddenly felt as though I didn't want to ruin the day by allowing a rain cloud to form over our heads.

"But it's very common," she said in a soothing voice. "And it is nothing to be ashamed of."

"I wish that were the case," I muttered.

"Have you talked to a doctor?"

I nodded. "I even started taking something, but it only got worse, and the sleeping pills he prescribed made me sleepwalk.

"I bet that was embarrassing," Clara said with a sympathetic giggle. Georgia must not have filled her in on my exploits.

I forced myself to smile. With everything Clara had been through in the last year, she didn't need to hear about the incident on the pond. The last thing I wanted was to add to her worries. "I stopped taking it, but, of course, now I can't sleep."

"It takes a long time to adjust," Clara told me. "You think that being a mother just comes naturally. Some of it does. The love. It deepened my relationship with Alexander. But that doesn't mean it's been easy. It's hard when you need a good night's sleep or the baby is having a fussy day or cutting teeth."

"How do you handle the rough days?"

"I remind myself that tomorrow is just as likely to be a good day as a bad one," she said. "And then I forgive myself for not always being a saint."

"You aren't a saint?" I asked like I sincerely doubted this.

"Trust me," she laughed. "I'm far from a saint. There are days when I don't want to do any of it. I just want to hide in the bedroom and pull the covers over my head. I probably could. Alexander has half of the Army around at any given time, some of them have to know how to change nappies."

"But you don't," I guessed.

"I take an extra five minutes," she said softly. "And then I get up and do my best to find as much joy as I can in that day. Sometimes it's only a single moment and the rest of it sucks, but that one moment..."

"Makes up for all of it," I added softly. I knew exactly what she meant. For every time I'd been unable to soothe Penny, there'd been a moment of looking down and seeing how much she looked like Smith from a certain angle or watching her smile in her dreams.

"That's why it's so important to have Alexander around," she confided in me. "Every time I see him with one of our children, I fall a little more in love with him."

A dozen images of Smith cradling Penny and rocking her to sleep rushed to mind. It was an amazing gift to see the man I loved with our child. "Sometimes I miss it just being the two of us."

"Of course you do," Clara said, not at all offended by my confession. "It was certainly easier to sneak off to shag.

But don't forget there were plenty of things dividing your attention before. The thing about having children is that it makes you realize your priorities. They come first, when it used to be your love."

"I know. I just worry that Smith and I will grow apart." In truth, I was worried we'd be torn apart. Every day seemed to bring a new test, and with taking care of Penny, that left little time for us to find to devote to one another.

"The secret is that loving your children is part of your marriage. Also, they don't stay little forever. You should see Elizabeth. I'm going to blink and she'll be off to university."

"Don't say that," I cried, wishing she'd brought her along, too. "I'm not ready."

"See? That's how you know you're doing just fine. The thought of the day where your house is empty again just makes you sad."

"I wouldn't mind a few more moments alone, though," I whispered.

"Well, you don't have to have sex in the bedroom," she told me seriously.

I pressed my palm to my chest. "How shocking, Your Majesty!"

"There's a lot of places to sneak away to at Buckingham." She shrugged with an impish grin.

It was always so easy to talk to Clara. I just wished we weren't so far apart everyday. "I just can't shake the feeling that I'm going to mess this up. That I'm going to mess her up."

"I saw you with Wills and Elizabeth. You're natural at

this, too. The stakes just feel a lot higher when it's your own kid."

"I hate to break up the reunion," Georgia interrupted, striding over and waving her phone. "But it's getting late. I don't know what the roads will be like when we head out this evening, but we should probably get going."

Clara's hand closed over mine again as Georgia went to tell Edward. "You can call me anytime. You can tell me anything. I know that sometimes between sleep deprivation and teething and lack of sex it can feel like you're going crazy. Just remember, I'm always here and I understand."

I nodded, reaching over to give her a hug. I wish it was as simple as that. Maybe my trip to London was what I needed to clear my head. No more sleeping pills. Different medication. And a reminder of who I was what I wanted.

Yes, London's always a good idea.

15

SMITH

I found Rowan adding a new lock to the Bless office doors. He stepped back and appraised it. "Too much wind," he told me. "It keeps gusting open. This should do the trick."

"Thank you," I said. I hadn't sought him out because of work, but rather to dig up more information on the history of Thornham. "I was wondering if I could ask you another question about the Thornes."

He shrugged, leaning to pick up the tools he used to add the lock. "I told you pretty much everything I know."

"That's actually what I wanted to ask you about." I'd been thinking about Rowan's information all afternoon. According to everyone in town, all of the Thornes disappeared. Even Longborn had seemed shaken when Miranda's remains hadn't been with the others. Despite the rumors that seemed to cling to her, it appeared that everyone assumed she was dead, too. In the way of country superstitions, people were just as likely to believe they were seeing a ghost as the woman herself. But if what Rowan said was true, they couldn't have seen her at all. Miranda Thorne had been locked away in an insane asylum. That left me with one more question for Rowan. "How did you know that she'd been institutionalized?"

Rowan turned, but his beady eyes focused on something in the distance. "That's not really my story to tell."

"I just want to find her," I told him. "Confirm that she's been locked away. Some of the things that happened since we moved in can't be explained."

"I told you that's always how it's been at Thornham. Finding Miranda won't help you with that," he said in a gruff voice.

"But how did you know that she was alive and in an insane asylum?"

Rowan chewed on his cheek for a moment as if considering how much of the story to share before finally sighing heavily. "I suppose it doesn't matter anymore. Not with Seth dead."

"Who Seth?" I asked, feeling confused.

"My brother. He worked here before me," he reminded me.

I nodded, hoping he would continue.

"He was several years older than me. Twenty-three and with plenty of Scottish charm," he told me with a wink.

"You can't blame a Scottish man for that," I agreed with him.

"You can't. And you can't blame a Scottish man for turning a woman's head — even a married woman's head."

I was beginning to get a better picture of life in Thornham years ago.

"Miranda Thorne was a beautiful woman," he continues. "By all accounts, she loved her husband desperately when they were first married. That's how they wound up with so many bairns. But sometimes love doesn't last forever."

"True love does," I said softly.

"I hope in your case you're right," he said with a shake of his head. "Maybe she still loved him. I don't know much. They grew apart. By the time I came to work at the house, the marriage was all but over. Then one night, there was a big fight between Mr. Thorne and Mrs. Thorne. Everyone on the estate was talking about it for days. Mr. Thorne left the house, and Mrs. Thorne wouldn't leave her room. The children were getting into all sorts of trouble, as children often do. Then little Caroline fell off the roof—I told you about that."

I nodded. He'd also mentioned that some weren't convinced it was an accident.

"When that happened, Mr. Thorne came back here quickly, and everything seemed to be fine—and then we showed up to work one morning and everyone was gone."

"That's when you called the police?"

"Not at first," Rowan admitted. "Everyone sort of assumed they'd taken the children off for a holiday. But when they didn't return that's when the local authorities got involved."

"They never found anything," I told him. "Not until we dug up the cellar."

"No, they didn't."

"Then how do you know Miranda Thorne was in an insane asylum?"

"Seth told me," he confessed. "He was the reason the Thorns had been fighting. Mr. Thorne had found out that Miranda had been seeing Seth. He caught them in the stables, actually."

I looked up at the whitewashed stable, an acid taste in my mouth. I couldn't imagine a future in which Belle would after cheat on me nor I on her. But I could imagine how infidelity could shake the core of a marriage. My first wife had been unfaithful to me a number of times. I'd done the same to her. I knew what it was like to love someone and then slowly lose all connection with them.

"She came to Seth and told him she was with child," Rowan told me. "*His* child. She was raving. Said she wasn't safe. The police were searching for her by then—searching for any Thorne they could find. He tried to hide her away at first, but then… Well, it became obvious to him that she needed more help than he could give her. He found a place in Brighton that would take her. That's how she wound up institutionalized."

"What happened to the baby?"

"What happens to babies born to institutionalized mothers? It was a long time ago," Rowan said. "Things weren't the same back then. I'm sure the baby found a home somewhere."

"And Miranda? She's still there?"

"As far as I know, she never left," he said sadly.

I understood now why Rowan hadn't been more forthcoming about his past with Thornham. His brother Seth had been intimately involved with the Thorne family. I also knew what it was like to want to leave the past behind only to have it rear its ugly head over and over. I thanked him and made my way back toward the house. I didn't believe in ghosts, but I did believe that the past could come back to haunt you. The question was: whose past was haunting us now?

I SAT IN MY STUDY, STARING OUT THE WINDOW AT THE large oaks that towered behind the main house. Their branches reached out as if to offer me comfort, or, perhaps, refuge from Thornham itself. I had found the asylum in Brighton where Miranda Thorne must have been placed, using my mobile. I didn't know what I would do with that information. What answers could I hope to find by seeking out a woman who'd been considered insane for decades? The more I learned about our house, the more I wondered if the country was the safe haven I'd hoped it would be.

The house was eerily silent. I sent Mrs. Winters off for the evening, determined to wait for Belle and the others for dinner. Penny had been napping happily in the nursery under Nora's watchful eye through the afternoon. Georgia had texted when they left London, telling me they'd be home soon. It was time to tell Belle what I'd uncovered. Miranda Thorne may have been locked away, unable to hurt anyone else, but there was another Thorne in the world—one almost nobody knew about. I didn't know whether to see that as conspiracy or coincidence, my own life too scrambled by the past for me to say either way. I leaned back in my chair, rolling my neck along its edge in a futile attempt to work out the perpetual tension locked there.

The soft footfall of approaching steps caught my attention. I stared out the window, watching the stars that punctuated the sky so brilliantly in the country. I promised to give her those, but what would it cost us?

"I don't know what to do," I confessed and I heard her stop. It would be easier like this. I had not wanted to keep what was going on from her. I didn't want to keep anything from my wife, but her fragile mental state seemed to dictate it necessary. Now that I had answers, it was time to come clean. "I swore I would protect Penny, but I can't help thinking that I'm failing her. Maybe coming here was a bad idea. There are things you should know. But I don't know where to begin."

I closed my eyes, pinching the bridge of my nose with my thumb and index finger, feeling another headache coming on. She came behind the chair, her delicate hands reaching to knead my shoulders. "Do you think anyone ever escapes their past? I can't help feeling like my sins have come to collect."

I reached up, closing my hand over hers to draw her down, needing her skin on mine, craving the taste of her kiss.

"Is that a new perfume?" I asked, bringing her wrists to my lips and breathing in the scent of her. "I like it."

I opened my eyes, starting to turn and take her in my arms when my gaze caught a reflection in the window. I dropped the hand of my mouth, spinning the chair around before jumping to my feet and taking a step back. Nora froze on the spot, her dark eyes round orbs against her pale skin.

"It's okay," she finally murmured, edging a bit closer. "You aren't failing anyone, Smith. Penny couldn't have a better father."

"You should leave," I growled in a low voice. Her perfume lingered in my nostrils, turning my stomach.

"I see you." She shook her head, refusing to budge. "Belle might not see how hard you're fighting—"

"Do not say her name." It was all I could do to keep my fury under control. Georgia had warned me and I hadn't listened.

"Smith," she said softly, daring to move closer to me and reaching to place palm on my chest. "I can be —"

I shoved her hand away. "You need to leave."

"If you would only—"

"Pack. Your. Bags!" I exploded.

She advanced again and grabbed a fistful of my sweater. "You've felt it, too! I've seen the way you look at me when she isn't watching."

"What the fuck is going on here?" Belle's voice sliced through the air.

Nora startled away from me, cringing into the shadows.

"Beautiful," I called, but she had already fled. I turned on Nora, taking one menacing step in her direction. "Clear your room. I want you gone in the morning."

"You don't mean that." She gasped. "Who will take care of Penny? You can't trust her—"

"Get the fuck out of my house." I didn't wait for her response. I was already out the door, heading in the direction Belle had gone.

Edward stopped on the stairs, his arms full of shopping bags, and moved to the side when he saw me flying down them.

"Where did she go?" I barked as I passed him.

"She came in to find you as soon as we got home," he answered in confusion. "What is going on?" I saw his eyes flicker up to where Nora had appeared at the top of the stairs.

I didn't have time to explain to him. I needed to find Belle before she got too far. Georgia appeared, laden with so many purchases that she looked like a pack mule, as I reached the foyer. She dropped the items with a grunt, looking exhausted. Her eyes narrowed as soon as she saw me.

"Did she go this way?" I asked.

"Who? Belle?"

It was answer enough. I switched directions, heading to the back of the house and finding the door wide open.

"Belle!" I yelled into the night, but she didn't respond. I hesitated only long enough to decide whether to go in the direction of the pond or her offices. She was angry—spitting with rage, I was sure—not sleepwalking, so I ran in the direction of the stables.

By the time I reached them, lights were flickering on in the space. I tried the door and found it locked. I banged on it with my fist. "Open the door, beautiful."

I waited for a moment. When she didn't answer, I

pounded harder. The door finally flew open to reveal her standing, hands planted on her hips and eyebrows raised, waiting for her explanation.

"That wasn't what it looked like."

"It looks like our nanny was trying to fuck you," she said flatly, crossing her arms over her chest with a look that dared me to contradict her.

I had better self-preservation instincts than that.

"And failing," I said, tossing a grin at her. But her lips only flattened more. She wasn't in the mood for jokes. I pushed past her, kicking the door closed behind me. There was only one way to solve this: I was going to have to prove it to her.

"What do I have to do?" I dropped to one knee at her feet, then the other. "Beg? Nothing happened and nothing ever will."

"Nothing?" she pressed.

My jaw clenched and I took a deep breath. "She came in when my back was turned. I thought it was you."

"What does that mean?" she asked in a strangled voice.

"She gave me a neck massage, and I...took her wrist and kissed it." I could still taste Nora's foreign scent on my tongue.

"You kissed her?" Belle whispered.

I opened my mouth to clarify once more, but somehow I knew it didn't matter where I had kissed Nora. What mattered was that my lips had touched another woman.

Belle paced over to the desk and stood in silence for a moment before turning to me. "Do you remember when Philip came to see me outside your office in London?"

My eyes flashed, and I nodded. "He wanted you back."

"I told him no, and he kissed me," she recalled the story.

"I'd much rather forget that ever happened," I admitted to her.

"I know," she said in a lofty voice, bringing her cautious eyes to mine. "But that didn't stop you from making me prove my loyalty when you found out."

I lifted the hand that wore my wedding band. The one she had placed on my finger. "I am yours. Nothing changes that."

"Prove it." She issued the challenge with a grim smile.

"Anything," I promised her.

She studied me for a moment before walking past me to the racks of clothing lining the far side of the office. She moved a few hangers, then reached to dig into the baskets of accessories below the clothes. Finally, she straightened triumphantly with a thin leather belt in her hands. Belle snapped her fingers and pointed to the ground below her feet. Then she said one word: "Crawl."

It was more than a challenge, she was proving a point. Belle had rarely topped me in the bedroom unless I allowed it. After all, how could I not appreciate watching her bounce on my cock from time to time. That wasn't what she wanted now. She wanted to remind me that for every moment of dominance I enjoyed it was due to her submission. She gave herself to me freely and with trust. She allowed me to claim her body according to my own dark whims, but she was always the one in true control. She alone held the power to grant her submission.

And now I needed to earn it back: her trust, her submission, her heart.

I kept my eyes on her as I rocked forward and placed my palm on the ground. Slowly, I crawled to her on hands and knees. I'd never thought I would lower myself to this for any woman, but I would spend my life in chains just to kiss her feet. When I reached her, I did just that.

"Very nice," she murmured as I placed a single kiss on the toe of her leather boots. Belle wrapped the leather belt around my neck, feeding one end through its buckle before tightening it. "Lovely."

She had collared me. The message was clear: I belonged to her.

I rocked back on my heels, waiting for my next instruction. She pointed to her thick, black leggings. "Pull them down."

My hands shot up to hook her elastic waistband and then I peeled them off her, revealing inch after inch of creamy bare leg until they caught at the shaft of her boots. Belle managed to spread her legs as far as her trapped legs would allow. Her pussy was bare save for a soft thatch of blonde hair. I licked my lips.

"Show me who you worship," she demanded.

I nodded, eagerly pushing onto my knees. I reached to grab her hips and bring her to me, but she slapped my hands away. "Use your mouth."

My cock felt like it might explode in my pants, but I had no other issue with this dominant side of my wife. I rather liked her demanding pleasure from me. I always wanted to give it to her. It was almost as good when she took it. I leaned carefully forward, planting my face against her sweet mound. It took concentration to part her with my tongue. Belle responded by wiggling a little farther apart to give me better access. I swept the tip of my tongue along her before moving to concentrate on her engorged clit. I moaned as her taste filled my mouth, erasing whatever sliver of Nora that remained.

"What's that?" she asked. She backed up a step, taking away her sweet cunt.

"I love having my mouth on you."

"No," she said harshly. She bent so that our eyes were level, and I wished I was behind her so I could see her round ass thrust into the air behind her. She grabbed hold of my makeshift collar and forced me to focus on her. "You love when I put my pussy on your lips, when I ride your tongue—don't you?"

I only had one chance to get this right. We were playing a game, but I was determined to give her the win. "Yes, Madame."

A smile curled slowly across her lips. "Good. I'm going to fuck your mouth until I come. Would you like that?"

"Yes, Madame," I repeated, turning my face up to welcome her to it.

Belle took a few more steps away, bent lower, and unzipped her boots. She slid off each one before removing her pants entirely. Then she walked to me, hips swaying side to side. I rocked back onto my heels, submitting my body to her as she straddled my face. "You may hold me up."

Fuck. I never knew she could be this hot. She might be

trying to prove something, but part of me wanted to pick fights more often if it meant she would take control. I grabbed her buttocks holding her steady as I buried my tongue inside her. I swept it over her clit until it was plump with blood before nipping it with my teeth. Belle crushed her pussy to my mouth, and I met it with hunger. Her hands tangled in my hair as she rocked roughly against me. When she came, her thighs clamped over my ears and she bucked out the aftershocks, moaning with pleasure as she slowly smothered me.

It would be the perfect way to go.

Still, when she moved aside, I gasped for air. She didn't seem remotely concerned. Instead, she pointed to the ground. "Stand up."

I licked the remnants of her off my lips as I did so. Belle pointed to the table I'd fucked her on only last week. I walked to it, painfully aware of my swollen balls. When I reached it, she circled her index finger. "Turnaround."

I did as she directed, wondering what she had in store for me next. Belle moved behind me, her arm slipping around my waist and down the front of my pants. She stroked it roughly, her dry hands burning with the friction of her frantic pace. "This is mine," she snarled quietly in my ear. Her other hand grabbed the tail of the belt and she yanked it until I could barely breathe. "Do you understand?"

I tried to swallow but couldn't due the leather restricting my throat. I blinked instead and she smirked. "You like it, don't you? Belonging to me."

She waited, but I couldn't move without cutting off all my air supply. Belle raised an eyebrow.

That's when I realized that it wasn't about how far she would take this, but how much of myself I was willing to submit to her. I jerked my head against the leather collar, cutting off my oxygen so I could give a full and unmistakable nod. Instantly, stars swam in the edges of my vision. My balls constricted and I released into her hand. Belle let go of my collar and I collapsed forward, my hands catching the edge of the conference table to stay upright. Her hand slid out of my pants and she lifted to show me her palm, glazed in my climax. I watched as she swept her index finger over it, coating the tip with my ejaculation. Then she reached and brushed it on my lips. I froze, my eyes locking with hers to find a challenge there.

I told her she had all of me. Now I had to prove it. Belle had never denied me a thing in the bedroom. I had a choice to make. My lips parted and she pushed her finger into my mouth, smearing my climax on my tongue.

"Taste yourself," she murmured. I sucked her finger, surprised to find myself growing hard again. It had nothing to do with my own taste, but rather the shameless confidence in her actions. "I love the way you taste." It mixed with the lingering flavor of her on my tongue and my eyes hooded as I swallowed the sample of our union.

She stepped back, looking pleased and the strangest sense of pride surged through me. Is that she felt when she gave herself to me? Her eyes flickered down to the erection poking out of the waistband of my pants.

"I never want your lips to touch another woman's skin."

This time the command had left her voice. She reached up and undid the belt at my neck. It slipped off and her hands rubbed the marks it left behind.

"You're not bad at this," I complimented her.

"I still prefer the other side," she said simply.

I arched an eyebrow. "I am sorry, beautiful."

"I know." But she didn't quite meet my eyes.

"How can I prove it to you?" I asked.

"You don't have to prove anything," she said, shaking her head. "I know."

"I think I better try anyway," I said gruffly. I lifted her onto the table and positioned my cock between her legs. Instead of pushing inside her, I waited. This was still her challenge. I would prove to her that I belonged as much to her as she did to me. She rocked forward, swallowing me with her pussy, and her eyes rolled back.

"Say it, Price," she begged as she rode my cock. "Tell me you'll love me forever."

I groaned, quickening my pace. "I'll love you forever—and a day."

16

BELLE

I wished I could sleep as soundly as Smith after what happened. He'd carried me back to our room and taken me again, putting himself back in charge. I hadn't fought him on it. I needed the reassurance after what had happened that he still belonged to me and that I still belonged to him. Instead, I lay awake in bed, staring at the ceiling. Smith was right to fire Nora. I'd never be able to trust her again—but that left us without a nanny. After my trip to London, I felt more confident as a mother. Still, that didn't mean I was ready to do it on my own. I reminded myself that Edward and Georgia were around to help, but I couldn't shake the slight sense of panic I felt.

Focusing on the panic was actually keeping me from confronting Nora and myself. I wasn't sure what would happen if I tried to talk to her now. She touched my husband— that couldn't be forgiven. Anger boiled inside me as the scene played out in my head, despite my best attempts to ignore it. I couldn't erase the image of her hand clutching his sweater as she tried to draw him to her. I didn't care what she thought about me. But I sure as hell cared that her hands had been on what was mine.

I turned my head and watched Smith for a moment. How had I not seen this before? How long had she harbored interest in my husband? I really was going to drive myself nuts soon. Carefully peeling back the covers, I slipped from the bed, doing my best not to wake him. Grabbing a robe from the chair near the bed, I tiptoed out and quietly opened the door. I needed something to clear my head. I tiptoed down the stairs, knowing all too well that between the marble floors and the wide, airy passages, sound carried. I didn't want my echoing footsteps to wake anyone up.

There was a light on in the kitchen, and I braced myself to find Mrs. Winters in there. But it wasn't her graying head standing before the refrigerator. It was Nora's. I stopped, considered what to do, and strode into the kitchen, allowing my feet to hit the stone floors hard enough to send echoes. It was my way of delivering a warning before I attacked.

Nora swiveled around, her hand on the refrigerator door. She shut it and slumped against it as if she was cornered.

"Stealing my food, too?" I asked coldly. I didn't give a damn about the contents of the fridge, but I cared that she was still here. Smith had given her until the morning to leave—a reasonable demand—but one that hardly felt satisfying. I had to resist the urge to kick her ass into the snow.

"Belle," she began before immediately falling silent. Apparently, the tart didn't know what to say to me.

I crossed my arms, allowing the silence to stretch between us until she finally filled it again. "It wasn't what you thought."

That was how she was going to play it? Did she think I was blind? I remained quiet. She would damn herself all on her own.

"Smith and I have been spending so much time together," she continued, "and he's been sending me mixed signals for a while now."

My jaw clenched, locking back the anger threatening to spill from my lips. I wanted to watch her dig her grave, and that meant not interrupting her pitiful lies.

"I got caught up in it. There's something about him that made me fall for him." Her head dropped with shame as her shoulders shook. When she finally looked up, tears streamed down her cheeks. "I didn't mean for it to happen. It was like I was swept under his spell."

"And he encouraged you?" I asked carefully.

"Yes." She hesitated and then shook her head. "No. I'm not sure."

"As long as you're clear on it." I couldn't decide if she was trying to save her own skin by blaming him, or if she really thought he'd shown interest in her. Either way, she was wrong. "Now let me be clear." I took a few steps forward, leaving only a few yards between us. Nora shrank against the fridge. "I don't believe you. Smith would never cheat on me."

"Maybe not before, but everyone knows you're not

yourself anymore." She rose up, getting an inexplicable burst of courage, and shook her head. "He needs a wife who can love him, and Penny needs a mother who can take care of her."

"You little bitch," I snarled.

"I'm not a bitch. I just see what you won't let yourself see. You've hurt him. You've hurt her. What will it take for you to see that you don't deserve them? This?"

"Could you be any more cliché?" I couldn't believe what I was hearing. Everyone had joked about hiring a beautiful, young nanny, but I'd had no reason to worry about my husband. It hadn't occurred to me that she might betray me. "I suggest you enroll in school immediately, because I'm going to make certain that you never hurt another family again."

"I need the money," she shrieked as if finally realizing the damage she had done. She took a shaky step forward. "I don't expect you to understand. Not with your mansion and your luxury cars and your ridiculous shoes. Some of us don't have that."

I was beginning to understand what had really driven her to make a play for my husband. I'm sure she did find him sexy—how could she not? But his money had to be at least as attractive. "I want you gone in the morning. We'll send your final check to the agency and inform them what you did." There was no point continuing this argument. There was only finalizing business. "Please be gone before we wake up."

"I want to say goodbye to Pen—"

"You won't go near my daughter." I finally snapped and

took a menacing step toward her. Jabbing my index finger into her chest, I made myself clear. "Or my husband. We will never see your face again once I walk out of this room."

I turned to leave and caught Mrs. Winters watching us from the back staircase. She said nothing before fading back into the shadows. At least, she had the sense to not get involved. I walked deliberately back to the stairs, counting each step to try to calm my pounding heart. Blood roared in my ears, and no matter how much space I put between me and her, I didn't feel any calmer. Instead of going to my bedroom, I went to the nursery to check on Penny.

She was sleeping on her back, her arms spread to her sides, fists clenched, as if she'd been preparing for a fight, too.

"I'm sorry," I whispered to her, my fury shifting to sadness. I'd put us all in this position. I had endangered her. I'd forced Smith to turn to someone else for help. A bottomless pit opened in my stomach, trying to drag me to the dark places I'd barely escaped. "No one will come between us. Not anymore. I'm your mother, and I love you. I'm sorry that I failed you before. I'm going to spend the rest of my life making that up to you."

Her eyes fluttered in her sleep, and she smiled softly, as if she understood me.

I checked the baby monitor and made my way back to bed. Smith was still sleeping. He'd shifted, throwing one leg out from the covers, so that his body was on display. I regretted making him prove his innocence. There was only one person to blame for this. I swallowed before making my choice. I had to be the wife he deserved. I had to be the mother Penny needed. Padding into the bathroom, I opened the medicine cabinet and took out the bottle of sleeping pills. Just for tonight. I watched myself swallow one in the mirror and promised my reflection the morning would bring a new day and a chance to correct the mistakes I'd made. I had to believe in second chances. I had to believe I could make this right.

17

SMITH

Light filtered through my eyelids, gently drawing me back to the world. I stretched my legs before rolling to the side and hooking an arm around Belle. I pulled my wife against me, shifting to press my cock against her backside. She squirmed in my arms, wiggling against my engorged shaft.

"Good morning, beautiful." I kissed her shoulder. I didn't know what I'd done to deserve waking up next to this woman every morning, but I would spend my life proving I deserved to keep her.

Belle turned her head, nuzzling against my neck. "Good morning, sir."

"So, I'm sir again?" I smirked and buried my face into her hair.

"For now," she said in a coy voice.

"In that case..." I flipped her over and moved between her thighs. Belle's hands slid up my chest, but as they reached my shoulders, her eyes widened. "What's wrong?"

I looked down, seeing exactly what had caught her attention. Beneath me, she began to shake, trembles rolling through her.

I sat up and she bolted up next to me, raising her hands. Our eyes locked for a moment.

"Smith," she said in a strangled voice as we stared at the blood and dirt smeared all over her hands, caked under her fingernails, and staining the sheets where she had slept.

I didn't think. I was out of bed and headed toward the nursery before I could process her calling after me. I heard Belle behind me, but I didn't stop until I reached Penny's room. Fussing noises came from the crib and I rushed over, lifting her into my arms to comfort her. Pressing her close, I drank in her soft scent, pressing my cheek to her warm head. I turned in time to see Belle collapse with relief.

"I don't understand," she said, her voice ratcheting in breathless panic.

"Did you sleepwalk again?" That might explain it, but it didn't explain the matter of the blood on her hands.

"I took a pill," she confessed softly. "I couldn't sleep after seeing..."

A horrible realization crashed through me. Belle gripped her wrists, sinking her guilty fingers into her flesh, her face mirroring exactly how I felt.

Her mouth moved, but no sound came out. Still, I recognized the single word she spoke:

Nora.

I carried the baby into the hall and spotted something I had missed in my mad dash to reach her: a trail of blood splattered on the floor. My eyes followed it, my heart stopping when it led to the nanny's bedroom door. I walked slowly toward it, cradling Penny carefully to me as I went. Instinctively, I moved as quietly as possible, hoping we hadn't woken anyone else in the house. Her door was unlocked and I opened it, bracing myself for what I might find. The room was empty. I walked to the bed and threw back the covers to discover more blood.

There was movement behind me, and I turned to find Belle sag against the door as she saw the scene in front of her.

"What did I do?" She asked in a hollow voice.

"We don't—"

"What did I do?" Her voice rose with panic.

I needed to get control of the situation before anyone else saw this. But Belle was already straightening, her body shaking, as she took a step backward. "I need to call the police."

"No." I spoke so firmly there was no way to misunderstand my command. "Take a shower. I need you to take the baby."

"Smith, I shouldn't." She shook her head at Penny in terror. "What if—"

"Do as I say, beautiful," I stopped her. I would take care of this, but first I had to find Nora.

It took me twenty minutes to convince Belle to take a shower. She was a hollow shell of herself, muttering a story about confronting Nora last night. I couldn't bring myself to ask her how that confrontation had ended. I followed her to our bedroom, determined to pull the ruined sheets off our bad while she cleaned up. She paused at the bathroom door and looked at me.

"I didn't do it," she said softly. "I couldn't."

I believed that, but it was clear she didn't.

"Everything will be okay, beautiful," I promised her. "For now, I need you to get cleaned up and then I need you to keep this a secret."

"But Smith —"

"Trust me," I said firmly.

Her shoulders slumped, but she nodded. She disappeared into the bathroom and a few seconds later I heard the shower water turn on. Penny was fully awake, watching me with curious eyes as I texted Georgia to meet me upstairs as soon as possible. It was a little harder to rip the sheets off the bed with the baby in my arms, but I couldn't stand looking at them a moment longer. I threw the down duvet onto the floor, followed by the pillows, then I yanked the sheets off with one hand. I balled them up and threw them in the corner. I would figure out what to do with it later.

I heard hurried footsteps coming up the stairs, and I went out to meet Georgia.

"What's going on?" She asked. "Does this have something to do with whatever trouble you got yourself into last night with the nanny?"

I pressed a finger to my lips and nodded for her to follow me. Before we reached Nora's room, I heard Georgia stop and suck in a breath.

"Is that..." She whispered. I didn't bother to confirm the

blood spatter. Georgia knew all too well what blood looked like.

We continued into the nanny's room and I gestured for her to take Penny. Georgia held up her hands and shook her head.

"Would you rather deal with this?" I asked in a low voice, opening the door so she could see the scene of the apparent crime.

She let out a low whistle as she took in the bloodied bed. "It wouldn't be the first time I dealt with a crime scene. Where did you bury the body?"

"You're not funny," I told her.

"I wasn't trying to be," she said flatly.

"There is no body." We stepped inside and I closed the door. Others would be waking up soon. "I need to make sure no one comes in here before I deal with this, but first—"

"You want to take a look around," she guessed. She sighed and held out her hands. Despite her earlier objection, she cradled Penny naturally. I'd known Georgia long enough to understand why she didn't like babies, but this was an extenuating circumstance.

Nora had begun to pack her bags, so most of her belongings were strewn into open suitcases on the floor. I bent down to pick up a notebook and spotted her computer peeking out from the rumpled quilts on her bed. I grabbed it, looked around for another moment, and said, "let's take this to my study."

I was careful to close the door to Nora's room. I'd have to be sure that Mrs. Winters didn't go in there today. I'd yet to tell her that Nora had been released from service, so there was no reason she should.

"We need to do something about that," I said, pointing to the blood spatter.

"Take your spawn." She thrust Penny into my arms. "I'll take care of it."

"Thanks," I muttered.

"It's nothing," she said. "Good friends are always there for you, but only best friends hide the evidence. Remember that, Price."

"What's going on?" Edward's voice interrupted. He yawned sleepily, messing his hair with his hand as he surveyed us from his bedroom door.

Georgia and I froze before sharing a look. "Nothing."

Maybe he was still half asleep, because Edward blinked, shook his head, and turned back to his room, muttering, "you two are weird."

"You're going to have to tell him," Georgia said.

"Probably," I admitted, "but for now we need to control the situation."

"Where's Belle?" Georgia looked around as if it was only occurring to her now that my wife was absent.

"Taking a shower." I clenched my jaw, feeling a surge of rage that this was happening.

"Why is she taking a shower?" Georgia asked slowly.

"Because she woke up with blood on her hands," I confessed to her in a low voice.

Georgia thought for a moment. "I better clean this up."

It seemed best friends also didn't ask too many questions.

I went into my study, my hands full with Penny and the items I had collected from her room. Placing the computer and notebook on my desk, I sank into the chair with Penny and opened the notebook. The first page was dated last fall. I scanned it, realizing it was a journal. There was nothing inside it but the empty thoughts of a young woman. I flipped forward, looking for when she came to live with us. I paused when I spotted the word interview and read the entry.

The Prices seem like a perfect couple. I think I made a good impression. I hope they hire me. I wouldn't mind looking at the husband every day. Not that I stand a chance with him. His wife is so beautiful.

She had been interested in me since the beginning. I thought about Belle's halfhearted objection to hiring a pretty nanny, and my chest tightened. We never should have invited her into her home. We never should have come here in the first place. I continued on. Most of it was mindless rambling, but around Christmas her entries took a turn.

I'm seriously worried about Belle. I don't think her postpartum depression is normal. Then again, what would I know? Smith is being so understanding. I hope she gets better soon.

I turned the page and read the next entry.

Belle went to the doctor. It's about time. No one trusts her with the baby anymore. She can't even remember the baby bag. I thought she was beautiful, but she's actually mean. I'm always worried she's going to yell at me. I'm so glad I'm here to protect Penny from her outbursts.

I polished and considered what she wrote. Belle was having a rough time when Nora came to stay with us, but I've never seen her say or do anything mean to the nanny.

I flipped forward, looking for what she had written about Christmas. She made a few entries about time with her family, but I wasn't interested in what she did while she was away from Thornham. I wanted to know what she had written about her return: the day we found Belle on the pond.

Belle is mental, and no one can see it. She's going to hurt someone. I'm honestly scared of her. I'm so glad that Smith won't let her be alone with the baby anymore. Today we found her walking on a barely frozen pond behind the house. Everyone thinks she was sleepwalking, but it's obvious that she's lost it. I hope the next time someone doesn't get killed.

I wanted to close the journal then, but I needed to see what she'd written about last night. However, when I thumbed through the pages, there was no entry. Only a missing page, where one had been ripped out. I pushed the notebook away and stared at it. The journal painted a different picture of what had been happening at Thornham. Was this how Nora saw things? Or was she blinded by her developing feelings for me?

I reached for her laptop and opened it. It came on and I was surprised to find a picture of Penny as her screensaver. Thankfully, it wasn't password-protected. I clicked on the icon for her email account and it opened to reveal her last few emails. There was one to the agency we'd used to find her. I opened it and read its contents, my stomach churning. Nora was smarter than I thought. She emailed them last night, explaining that I'd tried to take advantage of her and that Belle had asked me to leave. I continued on to the next emails. Most of them were junk, but there were a number of emails to a M. Welter. A perusal of them suggested she was writing to her mother. There were a few responses, urging her to be cautious when it came to me and warning her that married women could be jealous. It was hardly Grade A parenting. I closed the laptop lid and considered everything I'd found. It didn't look good.

I didn't believe Belle had done this. I couldn't believe it. It wasn't in her. But without proof of her innocence, all we had was evidence of her guilt. Belle wasn't capable of murder. But something had happened to Nora. Someone had done something to her. Someone who knew that there were problems at Thornham.

"What did you find?" Belle interrupted me with a soft voice. Her hair was wet from the shower, and she slipped into a pair of loose jeans and a T-shirt. I beckoned her over, and she came to me, taking a seat on my lap and placing a hand on Penny's back. The baby squawked and squirmed toward her. Belle took her, cuddling her close before turning sad, blue eyes on me.

"She definitely didn't think much of us," I said in a strangled voice. I made up my mind not to let her read any of the entries. It would only feed Belle's concern that she was a bad mother. "I know you didn't do anything to hurt her. But someone had to have."

"Mrs. Winters saw me last night," Belle admitted, adding, "When I confronted Nora."

"You didn't tell me that."

"I didn't think it mattered. But it's not like Mrs. Winters would hurt her. Remember how upset she was by the allergic reaction? If she wanted to kill Nora, she could slip more nuts into her food," Belle pointed out.

"She has a point," Georgia interjected. "Still, I wouldn't rule anyone out. Except maybe Edward."

"He definitely didn't have anything to do with it," Belle said quickly.

I sighed. We were getting nowhere. "I know that."

"Who else would want to hurt her?" Belle asked.

"Maybe it wasn't about hurting her," Georgia mused. "Maybe it was about hurting you. What did Rowan say Miranda told his brother? She said something about how they were out to get her. Maybe she wasn't crazy."

Belle looked between us, her nose wrinkling with confusion. "What are you talking about?"

"There's something I need to tell you, beautiful," I began slowly. Belle listened as I revealed what Georgia and I had been investigating this whole time. When I finished she was silent for a moment.

"That's what you've been up to? Why didn't you tell me?"

"I didn't want to add to everything you were dealing with," I admitted.

"Forever, remember? She whispered, so only I could hear. "You can't keep things like this for me."

"I won't," I promised.

"Do you want to share with the class?" Georgia asked dryly.

"You're right," I said, thinking about what she said. "All of this trouble started at Thornham."

"Well, what can we do about it now?" Belle sounded as though she'd already given up.

"We need to find out what really happened last night."

"How are we going to do that?" Georgia asked.

"By figuring out what happened fifty years ago," I said. I kissed Belle on the forehead, then I did the same to Penny. I would drag the answers from the devil himself to protect them. I knew what I had to do now. "I'm going to visit Miranda Thorne."

18

BELLE

I was not capable of murder. I've had a lot of self doubt the last few months, but of that much I was certain. A tiny voice pushed back in my head, reminding me of what had happened two years ago in the London hotel room. That had been an accident. It had been self-defense. I wasn't capable of actually hurting someone.

But I couldn't deny that I had taken a sleeping pill and that I didn't know for sure if I'd stayed in my own bed last night. Was it possible I had sought Nora out to punish her for trying to take my husband? For trying to take my family?

I wouldn't!

I'd planned it out as I fell asleep. I would call the agency and let them know she was no longer working for us and why. I would handle this professionally, even though her own behavior didn't warrant such consideration. But now she was gone, and I couldn't explain what had happened to her. I couldn't explain why I had woken up with bloodied hands and dirty fingernails. I'd wanted to go for a walk on the property to look for signs that I had been outside the night before, but Smith had insisted on leaving for Brighton immediately. Georgia had stayed behind to quietly remove any evidence of foul play. Neither of them would hear of calling the police.

But if something had happened to Nora, how would we cover it up? What if they were destroying the very evidence that would prove I had nothing to do with it?

What if they were destroying the very evidence that proved that I *did*?

I was so preoccupied with my thoughts I didn't hear Mrs. Winters enter the kitchen. I turned and startled, waking Penny, who howled at the injustice. "Mrs. Winters!"

"Who else would it be?" She scanned me as she tied her apron around her waist. "I suppose Nora is gone then."

"What?" I asked before remembering that she'd overheard me telling Nora to get out of my house. "Oh. Yes."

"I'll clean her room later today. I imagine you'll be wanting it for a new nanny." She peered over her shoulder with beady eyes. "You might consider someone a little older."

"Yes." I nodded in agreement. "I don't think we're going to look just yet, though. Smith and I have things under control at the moment. No need to clean her room out. I think she left some things."

Mrs. Winters pulled a pot out of the cupboard and placed it on the stovetop. "Then, I'll see that they're boxed up."

"That's not necessary." I searched for a reason to keep her out of Nora's room, but drew a blank. "I was hoping you could make a cake, actually."

"A cake?" she repeated. Whatever for?"

"It's Georgia's birthday," I blurted out. It was a terrible lie. One that would be undone the moment that Georgia opened her mouth to contradict me—unless I forced her to go along with it first.

"I'll have to go to the village. You might have mentioned it before now," she clucked, clearly put out to be left to do something last-minute.

"I'm so sorry." In truth, I was relieved. I would have sent her to the moon if I had to. Making a cake was easier. "I just found out it was her birthday."

"Who's birthday?" Edward asked, striding into the kitchen.

"Georgia," I told him quickly.

"It is?" He scratched his head as if he was trying to check his mental calendar.

"It is," I repeated firmly. "Mrs. Winters is going to make a cake. But we shouldn't make a big deal out of it, because you know Georgia will overreact if she finds out."

"Okay," he agreed slowly, shooting me a look behind Mrs. Winters back. He mouthed *what is going on?* Out loud, he asked, "Where's Nora?"

It was a fair question, given that I had told him only yesterday that I planned to spend today in the Bless offices. I glanced over at Mrs. Winters to find she was waiting for my answer with obvious interest. "I had to let Nora go."

"Is this about whatever happened between you and Smith last night?"

I grabbed him by the elbow and steered him out of the kitchen. "I'll tell you about it on the way to the village."

"We're going to the village?" he asked in confusion.

"For presents," I said in exasperation as though this should be obvious. This lie was quickly snowballing into a ridiculous to-do list. I couldn't talk with Edward openly here, though. Not without risking Mrs. Winters overhearing. Until Smith returned From the Brighton Sanitarium with answers, I couldn't rule out that Mrs. Winters knew something about Nora's disappearance. I could only hope that she had nothing to do with it. I wouldn't allow myself to consider what she might have seen last night. Smith might be convinced that I had nothing to do with it, but I had taken the sleeping pill. I had no way to prove that I hadn't had another episode.

Edward followed me to the nursery and watched me pack Penny's bag.

"I guess she needs to come with us," he commented, lifting her from my arms so I could concentrate on getting things ready. "What happened with Nora?"

I sighed and braced myself against the changing table. Closing my eyes for a brief second, I considered where to begin. But when I opened them to tell him the truth, I looked up and spotted the nursery camera Smith had installed in the corner. Without saying anything, I rushed out of the room to Smith's study.

Edward came after me, peppering me with questions, but I ignored him and went straight to the computer. It took me a minute to log on and then another to find the application that stored the videos. It was a long shot. I mean, sure, the audio monitor was on last night when I checked on Penny, and nothing had woken me in the night.

"You're beginning to scare me," Edward admitted while I scrolled through the footage.

"Give me a second." I found last night's footage and forwarded until I saw myself entering the nursery. That was before I had taken the sleeping pill. I watched myself leave before skipping ahead. According to the video, two hours later, I entered the room again. My heart plummeted to my stomach. I had no memory of going to check on Nora again. I had been sleepwalking last night. Edward hovered over my shoulder, watching the video without comment. As we watched, someone else entered the room.

Nora.

"No," I said in a strangled voice. Nora came over to me and placed a hand on my arm. Then I watched as she led me from the room.

"What is this about?" Edward asked in a quiet voice.

I swallowed, no longer feeling an ounce of hope in my entire body, and turned my face to him. "I think I killed Nora last night."

19

SMITH

Brighton Sanitarium was as cheerful as I expected. The old, stone building looked like it belonged in a horror movie. A wrought-iron fence surrounded the grounds, and the asylum loomed straight up as though reaching to escape. I took note of the bars on the windows as I approached, parking the Range Rover in the lot in front. The day itself was just as gloomy; the temperature had risen just enough to turn what might have been snow into ice cold rain. It battered down from gray clouds, leaving bullet holes in the last remaining snow from the holidays.

I peeled the name tag the man at the guard post had given me when I drove up and stuck it to my sweater. I opened the front door, entering a holding vestibule, and waited for an attendant to buzz me. I supposed it was a precaution to keep patients from escaping. A bolt clicked and I pushed open the main door with hesitation. For all intents and purposes, I was entering a prison. I ignored the surge of adrenaline that rushed through me as the door locked behind me, trapping me in this soulless place.

A woman in a prim, maroon suit walked over to me and stuck out a hand. "Mr. Price," she said, reading my name tag. "Doctor Fellows. I'm told you're here to visit one of our long term patients."

"Yes. Miranda Thorne," I said in a clipped voice. I didn't want to explain myself. I wanted to get this over with and get out of here as quickly as possible.

"And how do you know Miranda?" she asked curiously.

"I bought her house," I said with a grim smile.

"It's not common knowledge that she's here," Dr. Fellows informed me. "May I ask how you knew?"

"My gardener worked for the family. His brother was a friend of hers."

"Ah, Seth," she guessed.

"You knew Seth?" I studied her for a moment. She looked to be in her forties, not old enough to have been here when Miranda first came.

"Seth visited often. In fact, he was the last visitor Mrs. Thorne had." She led me toward a pair of double doors, pausing to swipe an access card. "I have to warn you that Miranda doesn't speak much."

"I just want to see her." I didn't know what seeing Miranda would prove to me.

Fellows stopped in front of a door and knocked before opening it. I was surprised to see it was unlocked. She poked her head inside. "Mrs. Thorne, you have a visitor." She moved to the side. "Please return your name badge when you leave. We like to keep track of them."

"That's it?" I asked. "Don't you need to lock the door or watch or something?"

"Usually," she admitted before glancing at Miranda who sat silently on the bed, staring at the wall. "But Miranda has been here longer than any other patient in the facility. Most people pass through our facilities for a few weeks or months. She's been here for decades, as you know. She's never tried to escape. She's never harmed another patient. She just sits in her room. Of course, she's quite heavily medicated. Anti-psychotics. They affect everyone differently."

"I see. I won't be long."

The doctor left, closing the door, as I lingered in the entry.

"Mrs. Thorne, my name is Smith."

She didn't answer. I couldn't imagine what it would be like to be locked away for fifty years, rarely speaking, never trying to escape. The woman in front of me didn't look insane. Her silver hair was neatly combed, her dress old-fashioned but clean. She didn't look up at me as I spoke, but remained seated on the edge of her bed with her hands folded in her lap. The room itself was as lifeless as its inhabitant. Walls, which had once been a cheerful yellow, had faded to the color of an old newspaper. The walls were bare save for a single cross hung in the center of the far wall. There was a chair and a bureau, but nothing else. No books. No art. No photographs. No sign that this had been someone's home for half a century.

"I was hoping you could answer a few questions." I

crossed the room, hoping my movement might inspire a reaction.

It worked. Miranda lifted her eyes and I stepped backward. There was nothing there. No sign that a person inhabited the body in front of me. It was like looking into the eyes of a corpse.

I cleared my throat, determined to press on. "I recently purchased Thornham."

Her cheek spasmed, but she didn't move. I couldn't decide if I'd imagined the reaction.

"My wife and I moved there with our daughter, Penny. I understand Thornham was in your husband's family for a long time." The second time I mentioned the house, her shoulders arched protectively up towards her ears.

"There have been some strange things happening," I continued. She was listening. I could sense it. Her hollow eyes glinted slightly. "To my wife and my daughter."

"You should leave." The words cracked from her like she'd opened a dusty, old book with a rigid spine.

"I'm sorry," I said, moving towards the door. "I was just hoping you might tell me what happened to you." I reached for the knob when she spoke again.

"Leave Thornham."

I turned to find she was watching me, her chest rising in quick, shallow pants. "Why?"

"They're all there," she said, her head swiveling back to the wall.

"Who?" I asked.

"My children." Her voice grew more distant, and I realized she was slipping away again.

"We found them," I said softly. "We found their bodies. They're dead."

"Oh no." Miranda shook her head, sending her hair rippling like melting ice. "No one is ever dead at Thornham, Smith, no matter how hard you try to kill them."

Hearing my name on her lips was like having a bucket of ice water thrown on my head.

"I spoke with Seth's brother," I forced myself to continue.

She whirled around. "Seth? He stopped coming to visit me."

"I know. Seth died."

"Maybe he's at Thornham now," she said, looking to the cross. "You might watch for him."

I swallowed. "I will. Mrs. Thorne, when you came here you were pregnant. What happened to the baby?"

"Seth took her." There was a soft sigh to her voice. "He took her to Thornham."

"No one's been to Thornham in a long time," I told her.

Miranda looked up, piercing me with her ghost eyes and smiled, revealing rows of rotting teeth. "That's not true, now is it?"

I peeled off the name tag as soon as I passed through the double doors, wanting to leave everything about this place behind. It crawled under my skin like a burrowing insect and I fought the urge to rip off my sweater and scrape it off me. I stopped at the desk, annoyed to find it vacant, and dropped my name badge.

"Terrible idea, Mr. Price," Fellows said, returning from around the corner. "Twenty years ago, a visitor took off his name tag when no one was watching and he wound up stuck here for a week until someone came looking for him. The orderlies thought he was a patient."

"Then I'm glad you saw me," I said tightly.

"I was hoping I'd catch you," she said, holding up a file. "I was wrong about Miranda's visitors before. She has had one other visitor. Curiosity got the better of me. I had to look."

"Who was it?"

"I'm afraid I can't say. But you can fill out an information request and we'll contact the individual if it's okay with her, we can release her contact information."

Fucking bureaucracy. There was always more tape to work through. "Why would I do that?"

"I assume you were here looking for the Thornes. The other ones, I mean."

"We found them. They're dead." I didn't bother to sugar coat this.

But, working in an asylum, Fellows was no stranger to death. "I always suspected as much, sadly. At least, her daughter is alive."

My eyes flashed to her. "The baby? The one she had here? The one the father came for?"

"I'm sorry." She clapped a hand over her mouth. "I shouldn't have said anything. You really must fill out the form, but I'm sure the individual will be happy to speak with the new owners of Thornham."

"I doubt it," I bit out. I started to turn toward the exit before reconsidering. "Dr. Fellows?"

"Yes, Mr. Price?"

"Take my advice and lock that woman's door." I didn't wait for her to respond. I needed to get out of her. Away from this prison. Away from the woman who'd once walked the halls of my home.

Outside the air felt fresher, but the storm continued to press down. I walked slowly to the car, despite the fat, cold raindrops hitting my skin. I wanted them to let them wash this place away. I waited until I'd driven a half mile down the road before I pulled to the side and called Georgia.

"What did you find out?" she answered.

"Miranda Thorne is insane," I said.

"I could have told you that. Is that all?"

"No." I closed my eyes, hoping that I'd found my answer and dreading that I had. "The baby? Seth took it."

"Rowan didn't mention that," Georgia said slowly.

"Miranda said he took it back to Thornham."

"That's impossible. This house was empty—"

"As far as we know." I no longer could pretend that there was a rational explanation for Thornham and its effect on people.

"Smith, there's no such thing as ghosts," she reminded me.

I placed a hand on the steering wheel and recalled Dr. Fellows's slip about Miranda's visitor. "We're not looking for a ghost. We're looking for her daughter."

20

BELLE

"But it's not my birthday." Georgia tied the rubbish bag she was preparing to haul from my bedroom.

Next to me, Edward stared at it suspiciously. "What is that?"

"It's better if you don't know, your highness." Georgia heaved it over her shoulder and turned her attention back to me. "Why the fuck did you tell her that it was my birthday?"

I was on the edge of an hysterical breakdown, and I couldn't get Georgia to play along. I pressed my fingertips to my temples and rubbed circles. "Because she wanted to go up and clean Nora's room," I snapped. "And I couldn't come up with a reason why that was a bad idea."

"And you couldn't just tell her not to?" Georgia asked.

"Have you ever tried to give Mrs. Winters an order?" Edward asked, coming to my defense.

I gave him a grateful smile. "It doesn't matter. You have to go along with it now."

Georgia looked as though she seriously doubted she had to do anything I said.

"Please," I tacked on anxiously.

"It's done now," Georgia informed me. "There's nothing left in Nora's room, so there's no reason to pretend it's my birthday."

"Cake," Edward said out of nowhere. "Cake is always a good reason."

I stamped one foot on the floor until they were both looking at me. "We should just call the police," I hissed. "I don't want to hide this."

"That's exactly why Smith left your phone with me," Georgia said, pushing past me to carry the bag—and the last of the evidence—out the front door.

"He what?" I patted the pocket of my jeans and realized for the first time I didn't have my mobile. "Give it back to me."

"No way, beautiful," she said in a saucy voice.

"You seem to think this is funny." I was on the edge of collapse. I wanted Smith to come home. I needed him to reassure me that everything would be okay. But even I knew that wasn't true. Unless he found Nora, I wouldn't be able to live with myself.

"I'm just trying to keep you from doing anything stupid," Georgia whispered. "Like calling the police or telling Mrs. Winters. We don't know anything yet."

"That's just it." I shook my head, wishing she understood me as well as she understood my husband. "We don't know that I didn't do it."

"You didn't," Edward interjected. He'd maintained this

stance since we'd watched the footage from the video monitor. In his eyes, I couldn't have hurt her.

"Are you forgetting what happened on the ice? The sleeping pills—I wasn't supposed to take any more. But I did, and now Nora is missing."

"You didn't have anything to do with that."

"What if she did?" Georgia asked him bluntly.

"You can't honestly think—"

She cut him off, "I'm not thinking about it. You two shouldn't be, either. Let Smith do some digging. Let me look into things. Stop jumping to conclusions."

I threw my hands in the air and marched off. "I'm going to check on Penny."

"When are we going to the village?" Edward suggested in a quiet voice, joining me in the nursery.

I watched Penny dozing in her crib. She'd managed to roll over on her stomach. I didn't even know she could do that yet. I'd missed so much of her first few weeks. I couldn't stand the thought of missing more of her life. But that didn't mean I couldn't live with what I'd done if I'd hurt Nora.

"She made it past your husband," Edward reminded me.

"That doesn't give me the right to hurt her. Fire her? Yes. Murder her? No." I choked back a sob. "Maybe I am crazy." I had just begun to believe I wasn't. I had thought I was turning a corner. Instead, I found myself right back where I had started. It felt like an unholy limbo, and there was no escape.

Penny lifted her head, blinking her eyes blearily, and

smiled to find us there. Edward took a step closer and picked up the baby bag.

"You need to get away from Thornham," he decided for me. "Let's go buy Georgia a fake birthday present."

"She doesn't want one," I said flatly.

"Then take joy in giving her one anyway. How often do you get to piss Georgia Kincaid off?"

He was trying to cheer me up or distract me. I appreciated the effort, so I went along with it. After all, how much time did I have left to spend with him?

Buying a fake birthday present for someone who didn't want one proved to be harder than we had anticipated. Perhaps, it was down to the meager selection in the Briarshead shops, or maybe it was that I didn't know Georgia well enough to pick out something for her.

"Maybe we should ask Clara what she got her for her birthday," Edward suggested as we stared at a selection of locally crocheted tea cozies.

"The only thing I'm sure she likes are guns and leather." I picked up a teacup from the display. "If she doesn't want a present, why are we worrying about what we get her?"

He shrugged, and Penny moved along with his shoulders. He'd placed her in a baby carrier so that we would have our hands free. Most of the shops in the village weren't suited to prams. Of course, that meant he'd been getting a lot of interested looks. I had no doubt there would be a picture on a tabloid by tomorrow morning of the Prince of England wearing a mysterious infant.

"Well, I don't think we should get her any of this," he said. "Should we try next door?"

I nodded. At the door, I checked the blanket we'd thrown over Penny, making sure it was tucked around her small feet. The weather was warmer than it had been the last few weeks, but the sky was darkening overhead. A storm was moving in from the coast and would reach us any moment. We needed to hurry up. As we ducked into the shop next door—a quaint bookstore—we ran directly into Tomas.

He feigned surprise at seeing Edward and pointed to the baby. "You could've told me I knocked you up."

"I don't think that's how this works," Edward said, grinning despite himself.

Thomas leaned over and air kissed both my cheeks. Then, he turned and laid one on my friend. "You didn't call me."

Edward looked over at me, sending an SOS with his eyes. I shrugged. "Don't look at me."

"I meant to," Edward said quickly. "We've been really busy at Thornham."

"Don't worry about it. It sounds like your aunt and my uncle are having a good time in Paris," he said.

"I haven't heard much from her," I admitted.

"Exactly," Thomas said with a wink. "That means they're having a good time. Well—" he held up a shopping bag "—I need to get back to the restaurant. I'll see you around?" He posed the question casually but I knew it was intended for Edward.

"Yeah," Edward said. Tomas ducked out of the shop and I immediately smacked my best friend's shoulder. He rubbed it gingerly. "Ouch! What was that for?"

"You didn't call him?" I demanded.

"I haven't really dated anyone," he said.

"No one expects you to move on this quickly," I began, but he held up a hand.

"I don't think you understand what I'm saying. I've never dated anyone but David." His Adam's apple bobbed, and I realized he was holding back tears. "I don't know how to do this."

I wrapped him in a tight hug. "I'm so sorry. I wasn't thinking. We'll figure this out together."

"If you don't go confessing to murder," he whispered.

"Edward, if I—"

"You didn't do it." He pulled back and smiled through his tears. "Murderers don't give good hugs."

"Is that right?" I asked, smiling despite the way my heart constricted at that word.

"It's a fact."

21

SMITH

I tossed my umbrella in the stand by the door and headed for the stairs, just as the lift door dinged. I paused on the first step as it opened. Mrs. Winters hobbled up, pausing when she saw me. Her hand rubbed her hip, which must be partially responsible for the scowl on her face.

"Have you seen my wife?" I asked, knowing that asking after the housekeeper's well-being would only elicit a stern rebuke. She was made of stern British parts and didn't like to be reminded otherwise.

"I expect that they're planning the party," she said wearily. "Although, I'm the one left to make a cake all day."

"Party?" I repeated. Belle hadn't seemed in a particularly festive mood when I'd left for Brighton, and there didn't seem to be anything worth celebrating, at the moment. Not with Nora missing and no clue who was responsible for her disappearance.

"Miss Kincaid's birthday," she responded, narrowing

her eyes like she didn't have the time to explain this. "I better get back to the kitchen and check the oven."

I puzzled over it the entire way up the stairs. I needed to find the others. When I met Georgia in the hall outside my study, I still hadn't figured it out. "Why does Mrs. Winters think it's your birthday?"

She rolled her eyes so far back in her head, they looked nearly white. "Because your lovely wife needed to distract her from going into Nora's room, and that's the genius lie that came to mind."

"Oh, okay." I didn't see the harm in the lie, especially because Georgia's reaction was the first funny thing I'd seen all day. I had to take levity where I could find it.

"I cleared out the room," she told me as I went to the nursery. I stepped inside and looked around before she added, "They aren't here. They went to the village."

"You let them go to the village alone?" I exploded.

"Did you want me to babysit or clean up her mess, Price?" Georgia crossed her slender arms over her stomach and glared at me.

Normally, I'd know better than to pick a fight, but today I was on edge. "Don't you work for the royal family? How is it okay to let a prince walk around with no protection?"

"That's not what this is about." She strode out of the room, leaving me to follow her. Unexpectedly, she went toward my study. As soon as we were inside, she closed the door.

"What's it about then?" I asked.

"Her. You want to believe she's okay—that she didn't do

it." Georgia paused and took a steadying breath. "We can cover this up—whatever this is—and *you know* that. It's not the first time we've had to deal with something like this. But you need to accept that your wife might have killed that woman."

"Belle wouldn't..." I trailed away, emotion choking my words.

"It doesn't change who she is," Georgia said softly.

I lifted my eyes to hers and admitted the last thing I wanted. "Doesn't it?"

I'd turned it over and over in my head on the way back from Brighton. I couldn't get Miranda Thorne's hollow eyes out of my head, or her grim warnings. She was batshit mental. That was clear. But it wasn't so much what she said but how she looked. Belle had worn the same vacant expression that day on the pond. I didn't believe in ghosts, but I couldn't look at this as coincidence. The last mother to live on this property had gone mad. She'd likely killed her family and buried them in the cellar. Was that what was happening to Belle now?

She felt like water slipping through my fingers. I kept trying to collect her, but I was beginning to see that was impossible. Was she doomed to share the same fate as Mrs. Thorne?

"We need to find the missing Thorne baby," I said, determined to refocus my energy on something I could actually control. "There has to be some sort of record. The baby was born in an asylum, for fuck's sake. What if she found out she was a Thorne and was upset that we bought her family home?"

Georgia stood across the desk, her eyes filling with pity. "Smith—"

"Please," I stopped her before she could tell me it was another dead end. I knew I was grasping at straws. "What choice do I have? I can't give up on her. I promised her forever."

"I'll help you find her," Georgia said. She squared her shoulders and I braced myself for what blow she was preparing to deliver. "There's something you should see."

She leaned over and pressed a few keys on my keyboard. My computer screen flickered on and began playing a video. It took me a moment to realize I was looking at the footage from the nursery.

"This was last night," she told me in a quiet voice.

I watched as Belle walked into the nursery and loomed over Penny's crib. My hands tightened on the arms of my chair, digging into its leather when Nora walked onto screen.

"No," I said under my breath. I forced myself to watch as Nora spoke to Belle and then pulled her gently away. "No." I turned desperate eyes to Georgia. "I don't know what I'm supposed to do."

"We'll start with finding the Thorne baby," she decided for me, her voice coated with an uncharacteristic sympathy. "Then, we'll figure out the rest."

"That could take time." I slumped into my seat, realizing that I'd placed all my hopes in a fantasy. The longer I ignored what happened, the more danger we were in. People would notice that Nora was gone. They would ask questions. Mrs. Winters had seen Belle fight with the nanny and then there was the email Nora had sent to the agency. When the questions started, we would be the ones they came to for answers. "We can't waste time on a wild goose chase. It could take us months to find out what happened. We need to focus on finding Nora—" I stopped short of saying body.

"It won't take months," Georgia said, scrunching her face. "I doubt it will take hours."

My eyes narrowed. "What did you do?"

"We have powerful friends," she reminded me. "I made a call."

I rose to my feet, blood pumping to my heart so violently I thought my chest might explode. "You called him!"

"He owes you, and if any one has the resources to track down what happened to some wayside waif, it's the King of England."

But I was only half-listening to her. "Call him back. Tell him it was a misunderstanding."

How could I cover this up once he was involved? The more people that knew what Belle had done, the harder that would be.

Georgia checked her watch. "Bit too late for that."

"What does that mean?" I asked, but she didn't need to answer. The windows of the old estate answered, rattling with the sound of an approaching helicopter.

As luck would have it—because she's a bitch as often as she's a lady—the helicopter landed on the front lawn just as Georgia's Porsche turned onto the drive. At least if she wasn't going to accompany my wife and her royal friend into the village, she'd sent them in an armored vehicle. The car slowed its approach, no doubt owing to the spectacle unfolding on the grass. Then it shot forward as though the driver was determined to beat the pilot of the renegade chopper to Thornham.

It was a moot point, because as the engines shut off and the blades slowed, Alexander and Brexton Miles each got out, tossing helmets on the seat, and started casually toward the house. I couldn't help wondering how much Georgia had told them about what was going on, judging from their leisurely pace. I'd watched Alexander run towards domestic terrorists with more interest. They clearly weren't overly concerned that my wife might have murdered someone.

The Porsche door flew open and Belle got out, staring at our approaching guests before turning reproachful eyes on me.

I held my hands up to let her know that I'd had nothing to do with it. Edward got out of the passenger seat more slowly. Belle's gaze had been accusatory, his was murderous. I groaned as I realized that Edward hadn't spoken to his brother since this summer when Alexander had admitted to killing David. What was Georgia thinking when she called him? We were completely stocked up on drama without adding more to the situation.

"I come with a present," Alexander announced, waving a thumb drive.

Behind us, Mrs. Winters loudly cleared her throat. I

turned to find her looking scandalized at the front door. Of course, she had heard a helicopter arriving. "I suppose they're here for the party? You might have told me."

She continued to grumble as she turned to head back to the kitchen. Alexander reached me, wearing a bemused smile. "Party? You shouldn't have."

"I didn't," I reassured him, reaching for the drive.

He released it. "Care to fill me in on why I was summoned to deliver information on some backdoor adoption fifty years ago?"

"That's a long story," I began, but before I could get far, Alexander's eyes fell on Belle. Or rather, her companion.

The brothers stared at each other, neither speaking. Finally, Edward marched into the house carrying a parcel, without so much as a backward glance at us.

"Shit," Alexander muttered.

"What did you expect?" I asked. "A parade?"

"I'll settle for a Scotch," he said in a strained voice, "and an explanation."

I tossed a look at my wife, who was carrying Penny slowly toward the house. Georgia walked over to meet her, Brex following closely behind. She couldn't be in safer hands. Belle shot me a small smile as if to give me permission to ask him inside.

"I can handle that." I shrugged toward the house. "Follow me."

22

BELLE

I'd never expected the nursery to become a social gathering place, but an entourage followed me upstairs as soon as we were inside the house. Someone had lit a fire in the hearth, making it as good a place as any to linger. Of course, I might not have concerned myself so much with the design of the living room if I'd known we'd always be upstairs.

"Honestly, this is shaping up to be the worst birthday ever," Georgia announced as I finished changing Penny's dirty nappy. Brex was lingering in the corner of the room, averting his eyes. Edward was rocking furiously in the glider. I hadn't quite decided if he was on the verge of losing it or already over it.

"It is not actually your birthday," I reminded her with a hiss.

"Play along, Georgia," she said, doing an impression of me. "Which is it? What girl would be happy about the King of England crashing her day and taking all the attention?"

"When is your birthday anyway?" Brex asked curiously. We both turned to stare at him. "Not the time. Sorry."

"You called Alexander. He showed up. What did you hope would happen?" I said to Georgia. I'd been filled in on the barest details since our arrival back at Thornham. Smith had uncovered more about the Thornes, and Georgia had, in her ceaseless wisdom and incredible narcissism, actually called the King of England to do a quick research project. The fact that Alexander had dropped everything to do it was the real surprise. There was already enough drama today. Not only did Georgia ignore the increased risk bringing the King here might mean, the worst part was that she hadn't stopped to consider Edward at all.

I glanced over at my best friend again. He was still rocking in the chair.

"They have to talk sooner or later," she whispered.

"Is that what this is about?" First, she had forced him to confront Clara and now Alexander. "Are you going to dig up David's body and make him talk to him, too?"

"Impossible." Georgia shrugged. "We never found his body."

I was pretty sure she could take me, or I might have tried to strangle her. What was another murder amongst friends?

I decided to switch tactics and turned my attention to Brex. "What did you find that was so important that Alexander had to come all the way here to bring it? Don't you have email?"

His usually bright smile dimmed, and he tilted his head

meaningfully at Edward. Out loud, he said, "No clue. Poor boy just told me he could use some fresh country air."

"He was just in Scotland," Georgia said flatly. "And I thought you were supposed to be in Silverstone."

Brex had been assigned to deal with transitioning Anderson Stone, the late King Albert's illegitimate son, to the public spotlight. Considering all the royal family had dealt with recently, I couldn't blame Alexander for being concerned for his estranged brother's safety. He'd taken a break from that new role to oversee my time in London before Penny's birth, but, as far as I knew, he'd returned to Silverstone after Smith and I brought the baby home to Briarshead.

It seemed Georgia had thought so as well.

"I...wasn't needed there," he said hesitantly. "Anders needed a little privacy."

"I'm glad I was informed," Georgia bit out.

"You've had your hands full," he replied.

I picked the baby up and backed up a step, wondering if I should leave them to whatever disagreement they were circling around. But before I could, something occurred to me. "Wait, but what about Lola? Did she leave Silverstone, too?"

My business partner had been enlisted to work on Anders's image due to her genius at handling publicity issues. She'd been in Silverstone for weeks now.

Brex cleared his throat. "Well..."

"Oh." I finally understood. "That will be complicated."

"Nothing's happened yet," he said quickly. "I just felt like Lola could handle him on her own."

Georgia's shoulders shook with barely suppressed laughter. "Brexton Miles, are you playing matchmaker?"

"I'm just giving them a chance," he said gruffly. His eyes raked over Georgia as he spoke.

This time I definitely wasn't imagining it. I tiptoed away, giving them room to talk or fight or whatever it was they did, and took the seat next to Edward.

"I didn't know he was coming," I said to him in a quiet voice.

His gaze remained on the hearth, his brown eyes reflecting the flickering light from the fire. "I got that when you said 'Who the fuck is that?' when you saw a helicopter on your front lawn," he said absently. "He probably killed your grass. You'll want Rowan to tend it when he leaves."

"Sod the grass." I understood focusing on strange, seemingly insignificant details rather than face huge, painful feelings. But Georgia was right. Edward couldn't ignore what had happened forever. "How are you?"

"I was never going to avoid him forever. He wouldn't allow it." He looked at me, pressing his lips into a thin line as he raised his eyebrows. "And he gets his way."

"I'll make him leave," I offered. "I don't care who he is."

One corner of his mouth lifted into a smile. "You need his help. Our family is good at getting to the bottom of things and…"

Covering things up. He didn't say it, but I knew what he was thinking. If I had hurt Nora, my ties to the royal family could help me get away with it. I didn't have the heart to tell Edward that if we found out I'd hurt her that I didn't want to hide it.

"Pardon me, ma'am," Mrs. Winters interrupted, and everyone turned to her, "but will you and your guests be wanting lunch?"

"I'll check with Mr. Price," I told her, doing my best to act like it was no big deal that several members of the monarchy and their bodyguards were in our house. Not that Mrs. Winters cared about the why so much as that she hadn't been warned.

I got to my feet and Edward held out his arms for Penny.

"Can I hold her?" he asked.

I passed the baby to him with a smile. There was nothing quite as healing as holding her when she was in a good mood.

Mrs. Winters walked with me into the hall, and I realized she planned to stick around for an answer. I didn't want her to overhear what Smith and Alexander might be discussing in the study. I waved her on. "I'll come down and let you know."

"Of course, ma'am." Her lips pinched together, angry to be dismissed.

Honestly, when wasn't she angry with me?

I waited until she'd reached the lift before quietly entering my husband's study.

Alexander and Smith fell silent instantly—until they realized it was me.

"Beautiful," Smith sent the word out like a request.

I crossed the room and dropped into his arms. "What did you find?"

"Alexander found some birth records. Miranda Thorne did have a little girl fifty years ago."

"What happened to her?" I asked, glancing at Alexander for information.

The king lounged regally in the chair across the desk, his elbows rested on its arms and his hands steepled in thoughtful silence.

"Don't know yet," Smith said. "We are waiting on adoption records."

"But you came all the way out here?" I directed the question to Alexander.

"I had other business to attend to," he said smoothly. "Plus, we should have the information shortly."

"He's not ready to talk to you," I said fiercely, my urge to protect Edward taking hold. Alexander did get what he wanted—*too* often, in my opinion.

"That's not the only reason I'm here." He directed the full force of his blue eyes on me. "I'm told you need my help, as well."

"What?" I shot Smith a scathing look. How could he tell him that?

"Georgia called him," Smith replied in explanation to me, "but I did confirm that we have a situation."

I searched his face, looking for the reason he'd betrayed me by bringing in an outsider.

"I owe you both," Alexander cut in. He swallowed, a flash of vulnerability marring his unyielding demeanor. "For how you helped Clara."

"She's my best friend," I said. I hadn't done anything out of consideration for him, but rather her.

"The fact remains," he dismissed my reason. "And I believe Clara would say the same. She certainly agreed I should come when I told her I was needed."

"Shouldn't you be with her?" I asked hotly. They were both acting like I was in as much trouble as Clara had been when she'd been abducted. But Clara had been the victim then. Something I wasn't.

"Norris is with her. She and the children are quite safe at Buckingham."

I envied him his fortress. He had complete faith in the safety of the walls that surrounded him there. We didn't have the same security at Thornham.

"Finding the Thorne baby is the answer," Smith said, shifting the conversation back to our problems.

"Why do you believe that?" I demanded, getting to my feet. "What could that have to do with Nora?"

"I don't yet," Smith admitted. His shoulders went rigid, a mask slipping over his face. It had been a long time since I had seen him like this. He'd worn this demeanor often when we first met. Then, we'd been under threat from a common enemy. It had turned me on then to see how far he was willing to go in the face of danger. It had been exhilarating to watch how he controlled a situation.

I'd given myself over to that control.

But things were different now. Promises had been made, and we had more than ourselves to worry about now. Seeing the beast he'd caged peeking from his eyes scared me. I knew he wouldn't hesitate to do whatever was necessary to protect me, but at what cost?

23

SMITH

By noon, Belle had spirited Edward away to the Bless offices. I had no doubt both of them wanted to put much-needed distance between the occupants of the main house. I'd taken Alexander outside, on the pretense of giving him a tour of the property, so that we could talk without risk of being overhead. The footage of Belle in the nursery last night had reminded me that it was too easy to trust a closed door, but the walls often had ears of their own.

We strolled past the gardens, still half-covered in melting snow, toward the valley that extended beyond the estate's buildings. Alexander was quiet as we walked until we reached an old oak that was normally a speck in the distance.

"Did she do it?" he asked, as though he'd been waiting until we neared this point to pose the question.

"I don't know," I admitted.

Alexander shifted his hands behind his back, his eyes scanning the distance like he might find answers there.

"Does it matter?" I asked.

"Not to me," he said pointedly.

"I would do anything for her." I meant it. "It doesn't matter what she did or didn't do. I promised I would protect her."

"You should come back to London," he advised, turning to survey my reaction. "It will be easier for me to handle things if we don't have to deal with bumbling local detectives."

"And if they find a body?"

Alexander looked out over my property before raising an eyebrow. "We'll find it first. Brex can oversee it."

"And if we don't find her?"

"Then it will be even easier to deal with—no digging required." He clapped a hand on my shoulder. "London is the best choice, and I could certainly use you there."

"I'm not certain that life..." Belle had cracked in the quiet of the country. How much worse would it be in the chaos of the city? "I'd need to consider before dividing my attention. I wanted to leave this life behind."

He smiled grimly. "A feeling I understand all too well."

What he didn't say lingered in the air: but we can't.

No matter what we did, this life always found us.

"I think I'll walk a while," he told me, tipping his head toward the house. "It's rare that I get away from any of them long enough to be alone."

I imagined that was true. Alexander always had an entourage. I suspected the only privacy he ever found was in his own bedroom. "I'll send them in the opposite direction."

"Smith," Alexander called before I got far. I paused. "I know we've worked together a long time."

I waited. I'd gone to him after his father's death. I had never expected to stay linked to him this long, but then I had fallen in love with a whip-smart blonde with red lips.

"I want you to know I consider you a friend. I know I owe you," he said, "but I want to be clear, I'm not keeping score. When you need me—when any of you need me—I'll be there."

I considered his words for a moment. I didn't have many people I placed in the category of friends. Finally, I nodded. "Same."

We parted with the understanding that we were more than allies. It would never be like Belle and Edward. This was a friendship forged in duty and a shared concept of responsibility. Few men could understand the way I operated—Alexander was one of them.

"Don't get assassinated out here," I advised him.

"I'll try not to."

Our friendship was already off to a strong smart. As I returned to the house, I considered the fact that he might be safer outside Thornham's walls than he was inside. I was so lost in my thoughts that I nearly ran into Mrs. Winters as she wobbled out of the pantry.

"Your lunch is ready," Mrs. Winters informed me when I walked into the kitchen.

"My lunch?" I asked in confusion.

"Your wife was supposed to ask you if I should make

lunch for you and your guests," Mrs. Winters said in an irritated voice. "She never bothered to tell me what you said, so I assumed I should. Should I wrap it up?"

The last thing I needed was to lose more help around the house. Belle had her mind on other things, and I couldn't blame her for that. "No, I'll round everyone up. I apologize for the confusion. It's been a stressful day."

"I imagine so with Nora leaving." She studied me for a moment, wheels turning in her eyes. "I'll have dinner ready at seven. I assume His Majesty is staying for the party."

"Ummm," I hedged. "I assume so, too." I didn't want to speak for Alexander. He probably wanted to get back to London. Like me, he didn't approve of being apart from his wife and children for too long. But we had unfinished business to attend to, which meant that he would be here until it was wrapped up.

Mrs. Winters started back toward the kitchen, but paused. "I almost forgot. A letter came to you from a messenger. I left it by the door." She shook her head, looking disgruntled that she'd had to attend to this. "When will Humphrey be back from holiday?"

"This weekend, I think," I said absently. I wasn't expecting any deliveries. I no longer had clients to see to. We had purchased Thornham outright. I couldn't think of a single reason for a messenger to deliver a letter today. I turned, grinning despite the stress I felt, imagining what it must have been like for someone to bring a delivery and see a helicopter on the lawn. It was more surreal than amusing. I thought my life was complicated before I met Belle. I had no idea how much more complicated it could become.

I found the envelope sitting on a table near the entrance, next to an elaborate arrangement of fresh white roses and lilies in a silver vase. As I reached for it, the scent of the flowers hit my nose. They smelled cloying, and I grimaced.

They smelled like Nora's perfume.

I pushed against the memory of her touch. Of kissing her wrist. It had been a mistake—one she had paid dearly for. Belle had been getting better. I'd finally had some hope after she'd stopped the sleeping pills that we could make our life in Thornham work. But Nora had robbed that hope from me. She was a thief, trying to steal my heart, but all she had done was steal my wife. I had to make Belle see reason. Every time we discussed what happened, I saw the shame in her eyes. She wanted to turn herself in. She was scared of herself.

The worst part was that I was scared of her as well. Scared that she might vanish like Nora in the night. Scared that her mind was slipping away like Miranda. I knew she didn't want to believe that the Thorne baby had anything to do with this, but I needed to. The alternative was too disturbing to consider. Belle had not fallen victim to the darkness of Thornham. I couldn't believe it. Not without more proof.

I carried the envelope to my office and found my letter opener on the desk. Sliding its edge under the flap, I cut it open. I dropped the letter opener and drew out a single sheet of paper. A few photographs had been attached to its corner with a paperclip. My eyes scanned the printed letter, typed in a boring font that must have come preinstalled on whatever computer it had been written on. By the time, I had reached the second line, my pulse was pounding so hard in my ears that I felt as though I'd been sucked into a vacuum of space and time.

Darling,

I hope you've enjoyed our little game. We always had so much fun together, but then you got a new partner. Was I so easy to replace?

She was hardly a match for me. I can't imagine that she's kept you as entertained as I did. One more move, and I'll crush her completely. So I'm offering you a chance to take her place before I make my final play. Who do you want me to take off the board: the knight or the pawn? Deliver your response in person at the pond, at 7 o'clock this evening, or the rest of my portfolio will find its way in the hands of people who will lock her up for good. Only one player, please—fair is fair.

-M

My fingers fumbled for the photographs attached to the letter, my brain refusing to process what I should have seen all along. The first was a still of Belle and Nora on the security feed. The next one of Belle sleeping. My blood rose as I spotted my own form next to my wife. I had been right there when it was taking. But the last picture turned my bones to ice: Penny sleeping in her crib.

It wasn't a choice. It was a threat. One of us had to take the fall for Nora's murder. One of us had to admit defeat. It was an easy call to make. I was never meant to have this life, but, at least, I would finally be able to set my wife free from the veil of madness that had been thrown over her head.

The Thorne baby. Belle. All traps laid to slow me down. My enemy had been distracting me while setting up the final board. Now that an audience was gathered, it was time to stage my final defeat. I should have known all along that my sins would cost me Belle. Believing in love, in salvation, had left me vulnerable to an opponent I had never seen coming.

24

BELLE

"You can't avoid him forever," Edward reminded me. He placed a stack of design books on an empty shelf while leveling a serious gaze at me. He'd managed to convince me to spend some of the frantic energy building inside me on doing something productive. Smith had seen to finishing the interior of the Bless offices, but only I could put on the finishing touches.

But my heart wasn't in it. I didn't see a point.

"I won't." It was better to leave it at that. I'd seen the look in Smith's eyes earlier—I didn't know what he was planning, but I suspected I wouldn't like it. He had shut me out before when he felt he had to take matters into his own hands. "I don't know how to stop him."

"I'm guessing he would say the same about you. I don't know how you two wound up together. You're both too stubborn," he said.

I paused, resting against the desk Smith had only given me over Christmas. I was supposed to be starting a new life here. He'd given me this space to build Bless, and now I never would. "I don't know why we're bothering with any of this."

Edward continued finessing a frame on the wall, ignoring my point entirely. He didn't bother to turn around as he shook his head. "Because you have an empire to run. A few weeks ago, you were worried about going to Paris and scaling up operations to meet demands," he said. "Why don't you focus for a little while on how much you've accomplished?"

"Because it doesn't feel like much of an accomplishment at the moment," I admitted. "What does it matter if I'm behind bars?"

"Alexander won't let that happen." It was the first time that Edward had said his brother's name since his arrival.

"Now you're on their side?" I flicked the end of the pencil, sending it rolling onto the floor.

"I am always—and have always been—on your side," he said firmly. "But trust me, sometimes we are our own worst enemies."

"And this is one of those times?" I guessed.

"Promise me that you aren't planning to sneak away and turn yourself into the police." He moved in front of me, forcing me to meet his eyes. When I didn't speak, he clicked his tongue on the roof of his mouth. "That's what I thought. They aren't going to let that happen. I'm not going to let that happen."

"What about what I want to happen?"

"Do you remember that time that I wanted to wear Gucci to the Ambassador's Ball?"

I nodded. He'd decided that a statement needed to be made, but, actually, he was tired of wearing tuxedos. "I would never have let you go through with that."

"Exactly." He reached down and took my hands in his. "It's my job, as your best friend, to keep you from making stupid mistakes."

"Really?" I arched an eyebrow, but didn't pull away from his grasp. "Because I've made a lot of stupid mistakes lately."

"Well, I can't be around all the time," he teased. "You'll just have to stop sleepwalking."

And murdering people, I thought miserably. I was about to say it out loud when Smith walked through the door. Edward glanced between the two of us before dropping my hands.

"Mrs. Winters made lunch," Smith told us in a clipped tone. "You better head inside before she explodes."

I straightened to follow Edward, but Smith caught my hand. "A moment, beautiful?"

Edward paused as he waited for a signal from me. I nodded once, so that he knew it was okay to go.

"I'm sorry," Smith said as soon as the door closed behind Edward.

I flinched, physically surprised that he'd come to apologize.

"Why are you looking at me like that?" He asked when I continued to stare.

"I'm trying to decide if you're really my husband."

"I can admit when I'm wrong," he said defensively.

I raised the other eyebrow.

"I'm just rarely wrong," he added, smirking. The wicked grin spread over his face easily, but it stopped before it reached his eyes.

"Is everything okay?" I asked in a soft voice. He could claim that he was comfortable admitting when he was wrong, but we both knew that wasn't true. The fact that he had sought me out to tell me told me I had more to worry about setting things right with him.

"I don't want you to waste time worrying that I think you hurt Nora. I know you didn't."

"You can't—" before I could tell him what we both knew that wasn't true, his mouth was on mine. There was an urgency to the kiss. I recognized it for what it was: he was claiming me just as I had done yesterday.

I had driven him to this. But although part of me thought I should push them away and force him to talk this out, more of me craved the comfort I would find in his possession.

Smith carried me to the wall, our hands working to remove our clothing as we went. I tugged his sweater over his head, my fingers fanning over his hard pecs. He paused, momentarily lowering me to the ground to yank off my pants before hoisting me up. I reached to my shirt and lifted it over my head as my heels helped him push his jeans low enough to free his cock. He pushed inside me, meeting no resistance. I was too wet at the promise of feeling his skin on mine. My fingernails sank into shoulders and I clung to him as we guided each other to the answer that always made sense.

We had each other. We had our love. No one could take that away. No sin could break us.

Smith pressed his slick forehead to mine, panting, as he urged me higher and higher. "I love you, beautiful."

I was too close to speak, my mouth finding his when my words failed me. They promised him what I knew to be true. Our love would find away just like we had found each other. I shattered in his arms, safe in the knowledge that he would put me back together.

SMITH

Belle's lie had unintentionally paved the way for me to easily slip from the house while everyone else was distracted. I thought of the letter and the timing of the meet. Was it a coincidence or did my enemy know every step I took inside my own home? Did she know about the party happening inside my home this evening? She had pictures of me and my family. She'd been in my daughter's room. She'd watched the footage from the nursery monitor. It was possible she'd chosen the appointment feeling safe in the knowledge that I could get away, unnoticed, while the others pretended to celebrate.

But if she knew that, then she also knew that I wasn't alone at Thornham. I had guests. Powerful guest. Dangerous guests. Her threats were enough to motivate me to go before she changed her mind about granting me my move. If she slipped away, leaving her trail of bloody breadcrumbs for the authorities, I didn't know what would happen. Alexander could try to cover it up, but how long would the country tolerate high-handed behavior by the monarchy?

As much as I hated to admit it, there was one more consideration weighing on me.

I needed to see for myself.

I needed to face my ghost.

"Sneaking away from my party, Price?" Georgia's voice caught me as I stepped out the door. "I'm hurt."

I paused before tipping my head to the dark night outside. "I'll be right back."

I moved to step out, hoping she wouldn't ask more questions, but Georgia was too shrewd for that. "You're lying."

"What am I going to do? Walk until I find the world's edge and fall off?" Swiveling back to her slowly, I raised my shoulders as if to point out how ridiculous she sounded.

Georgia crossed to me, never taking her eyes off me as she moved. "Where are you really going?"

I didn't want her to be involved. I didn't know yet what to expect. I wouldn't know until I faced her and understood what had happened. Still, Georgia knew me too well to believe I was going out for a breath of fresh air. She wouldn't drop this, and the last thing I wanted was her to draw attention to my absence. I gestured for her to join me outside.

Night had fallen, the sky a black cloak over the countryside. A plume of smoke rose from the chimney in the living room, filling the crisp air with the smell of woodsmoke. I smiled, knowing Belle and Penny were inside, warm and safe beside it, surrounded by friends.

Georgia sauntered out, narrowed eyes watching me the whole time. Despite the chilly January evening, she showed no sign of discomfort in her thin blouse. "What's going on?"

"I got a note," I confessed in a low voice. I took the folded paper from my pocket and handed it to her. "Along with photos taken from inside the house."

Georgia took a step toward the house where a security light had flipped on after dark. She scanned the letter, interest turning to confusion and finally shock. Her mouth hung open when she looked back up at me. It took a lot to ruffle Georgia Kincaid. If anything could, it would be this.

"It can't be," she said, shaking her head.

"Who else, though?" I plucked the letter from her fingers and folded it back up. "I have to go."

"Not alone," she said defiantly.

"Yes, alone." I stepped before her, meeting her eyes under the light. "I don't know how this is going to go down. I do know that if this is a game, it will be too easy to pin this on Belle. It's what she wants. I can't let that happen.

"The note proves—"

"What?" I snapped. "I could have written it! I could have taken those pictures. They won't prove Belle's innocence at all. If I knew what evidence had been planted, if I could control the narrative, maybe we might stand a chance."

"Ask—"

"No," I cut her off. I knew what she wanted me to do. But this was about more than covering up a frame job. "I have to take care of this."

"What will she do with you?" Georgia asked. "Do you want Penny to grow up without a father?"

My jaw tightened, and I turned to find the moon. "When I was little my dad told me there was a man up there. That the moon was made of cheese. It's one of the few memories of my father that makes me smile."

"All the more reason to give Penny more memories of you," Georgia said softly.

"That's just it. I remember other things about my father. Meetings with scary men. Him making my mother cry. Being told to go to my room and not make a sound. His body, floating in that fucking pool. I have plenty of memories of my father, Georgia. Horrible memories of a cruel man."

"You aren't anything like him," she said. She grabbed my arm until I turned back to her.

"But will I be?" My question echoed into the night. "He told me about the man on the moon when I was little. It wasn't until I was older that he broke my heart."

I wouldn't put Penny through that. I wouldn't allow my past to hurt Belle again. She'd suffered enough for my sins. There was only way to be certain she never bore the weight of my past again.

"And letting her win?" Georgia challenged, her brown eyes flashing. "How does that ensure this stops?"

"That's where you come in. I left an envelope with instructions for you. There's also one for Edward and Alexander. And one for Belle."

"You're not coming back," she said in a hushed voice.

"I'm just covering my bases." I forced a smile, but we

both knew a lie when we heard it. "Look, just keep this quiet until it plays out—until I know what I'm up against."

Georgia nodded, looking unhappy at the request. But we'd been loyal to each other for years. She wasn't going to betray me now no matter how much she disagreed with me. She bent and reached into her boot to pull out a small pistol.

"Take this."

I shook my head, refusing to take the gun. Tonight, I was bringing a different weapon. One that would free us from all of this forever. "If I don't come back, give her that letter and tell her—"

"Tell her yourself." Georgia poked a finger into my arm. "I'll let you go. I'll hand out your fucking letters but I won't say goodbye for you."

I nodded. It was a fair response. I'd told Belle how I felt in the letter. I'd included another for Penny for when she was old enough to understand. If I could have ripped my own heart out and left it to comfort them I would. Instead, words would have to do.

Still, it had been easier to leave those letters and walk out the door than it was to face my friend now. I'd been able to divorce myself from my actions to this point, compartmentalizing my goodbyes into a checklist. Belle hadn't known what drove me to her this afternoon. She thought we were simply making up. The letters had been difficult to write but not as much as facing their recipients. I knew that now as I faced one. "Georgia, I—"

"I'm not saying goodbye to you," she cut me off. "And I don't want to hear your goodbye, either."

Georgia pivoted away, her boots crunching on the evening frost as she returned to the house. I watched her go back to the life I'd fought for and the family I'd made, back to the warmth and light and love I would do anything to protect—even if it meant sacrificing myself.

Then, I turned toward the night to do just that.

I used the flashlight on my mobile phone to guide me toward the pond. The security lights perched on the corners of Thornham didn't extend this far onto the property. It was probably why she had chosen this spot. But I suspected it had to do with that terrible moment a few weeks back when Belle had nearly fallen through the frozen lake. Since the letter had arrived this afternoon I had more questions than before. It was comforting to know that answers were near, even if they were going to cost me so much.

Fog had formed, blanketing the estate in a thick haze that made it impossible to see more than a few feet ahead. Part of me wondered if I'd made a mistake, refusing the gun from Georgia. But now that I was out here, I knew that it would have done me no good. I wouldn't be able to get a clean shot off unless I was face to face with her. The flashlight's beam, my only weapon against the fog, brought the trees around the pond into relief as I approached it, their branches' shadows barely etched into the dark night. Most of the snow had melted over the warmer afternoon. But now, as the temperature dropped, it had begun to refreeze, turning the untended wild grasses surrounding the water to rise like shards of glass from the ground. Light glinted off the blades as they cracked underfoot. It hadn't stayed cool enough for the pond to freeze over again. It had started to, but as I cast my beam across it I saw a dark patch at its center where it had yet to form ice.

A twig snapped on my left, its assassination echoing in the air around me. Whipping toward the sound, I raised the flashlight as she stepped from behind a tree and cut a path through the mist hovering over the grounds. Her head was bowed, her dark hair curtaining her face. A vice gripped my heart, waiting for her to look up. It was time to confront the ghost of the woman I'd never really known—the ghost of the woman I'd once thought I'd loved.

It was time to face Margot.

26

BELLE

The fake party was going better than most real parties I'd attended recently, likely owing to the two large bottles of scotch that Smith had delivered between dinner and the serving of cake. Mrs. Winters had fussed over everyone, looking quite out of sorts to be forced to attend the festivities herself. I picked up a bottle and poured a double into a tumbler and carried it to her. "Why do you have a drink? It's a party."

She turned flustered eyes on me, her cheeks already pink, and I smelled proof she'd already begun to take my advice. "I shouldn't. I need to get to the cake."

"Do you need help with that?" I asked as she shifted dangerously from heel to heel.

She looked scandalized by the suggestion. "I'll only be a few minutes."

She bustled out of the room, nearly knocking into Georgia as she returned to the party.

"What's wrong with you? This is your party," I told her, as she got closer.

"Have they been like this all night?" She asked, frowning as she surveyed Edward and Alexander. The brothers had taken up spots on either side of the room, placing as much distance between themselves as possible. Despite the caution, Edward glowered in his older brother's direction as he nursed what, by my count, was his third drink of the night.

"I probably shouldn't have asked them to be in the same room," I admitted. "Hopefully, Alexander will hear something soon. I don't think they'd survive being under the same roof for an entire night."

"He should probably head back toward London," Georgia said in a flat voice.

I tried to get a better look at her, concerned that I pushed this charade too far. Shifting Penny to my other shoulder, I turned to her. "We just need to liven things up," I decided, and clearing my throat, I raised my voice and called, "Time for presents!"

Maybe it was actually me who needed the distraction. Each moment without answers only reminded me that I knew exactly who was to blame. Myself. As strange as this night was, I knew there were no parties or evenings with friends in my future. Maybe I had subconsciously chosen my lie to leave my family and friends with the happiest memory possible, given the circumstances.

My announcement had its intended effect, because Edward rose immediately to retrieve the wrapped package we'd picked up in the village earlier today.

"You got me a present?" Georgia muttered quietly.

"Trust me, it's not much. We had a very limited selection to work with."

"Should we wait for Mrs. Winters?" Georgia asked dryly. "Isn't this all for her benefit?"

"Just open the present," Edward said impatiently, thrusting it into her hands.

Georgia pulled back the taped edge of the wrapping carefully before efficiently removing it in one pristine sheet. When she turned to place it on a side table, she looked up to find us all watching her with wonder. "What?"

"Nothing," I said quickly. "We just want to see what you got." I suspected none of us had ever seen her be so gentle with anything. What were the chances she had a soft spot for wrapping paper?

Georgia turned the book over in her hands and stared at the title, stamped in gold gilt. "The Art of War by Sun Tzu—I've read it."

"You have?" I did a terrible job of hiding my surprise.

"I can read," she said, sounding a little offended. Despite her objections to the fake party, she looked oddly moved by the gift. Georgia turned her head as if she needed to hide her face. I looked to the others, finding them as shocked as me.

"Thanks," she gritted out, still not looking at us. "I'll have to have a fake birthday more often."

The shrill ring of a phone distracted us from the awkward moment. Alexander pulled his mobile from his pocket and held up a finger. "Excuse me a moment."

My heart rocketed into my throat, beating so hard I was worried I would wake Penny. She had only just fallen asleep, what with all the unexpected excitement of the evening. I almost envied her. I wished I could relax. Alexander stepped out of the sitting room and left the rest of us to stare at one another expectantly.

Brex finally broke the uncomfortable silence. "How about a real birthday? On the actual day? We can have cake and presents."

Georgia's answering grin was grim rather than grateful. "I don't celebrate my birthday. I never have."

"Since you were a kid?" Edward asked innocently.

"Ever." She frowned.

"But it's not like this is your first party," I said with a nervous laugh.

"What if it is?" She shrugged her narrow shoulders.

I forced the startled look off my face, but it was too late. Brex and Edward were wearing similar expressions.

"Don't feel sorry for me," she demanded. "Who wants to celebrate the day they were born? You don't even remember that day! You might as well pick some random Tuesday and have cake then."

I'd hit up against Georgia's protective shell before. But, in recent months, I'd gotten a peek at the soft heart she hid under it. I made a mental note to ask Smith about her past. Surely, she couldn't have gone her whole life without a birthday party. Then again, Georgia liked to pretend she didn't need anyone or anything, especially when it came to her feelings. Most of the time, she didn't seem to have any at all. It was one of the reasons that I found her so hard to understand. I knew, for a fact, that she was a submissive, in the truest sense of the word. As someone who craved the liberation of giving control to my husband in the bedroom—if nowhere else—I knew the bliss that came with releasing the emotions and worries that preoccupied me.

But Georgia never seemed worried or upset about anything. Angry? Yes. But I didn't see how that equated to her sexual predilections.

"Stop dissecting me," she barked.

I turned away, embarrassed to be caught staring. "I'm sorry. I was just thinking..." I searched for an excuse that would give us both an easy out. Before I could find one, Alexander reappeared in the room, looking stricken.

"We should talk," he said in an unusually concerned voice. "Somewhere private."

"I think you can tell anyone in this room," I said, trying to ignore the slight shake in my own voice. "They'll all find out, eventually."

"It's not that—" Alexander cut himself off as Mrs. Winters entered the room. He stayed silently as she surveyed all of us and inquired about drinks. He didn't say anything until she headed back to the kitchen. "Where's Smith? I should talk to him, too."

"I thought he went to the loo." My forehead wrinkled when I realized I had no clue how long my husband had been absent. I'd thought nothing when he'd excused himself for a moment after dinner, but I'd been too preoccupied to notice his absence.

"You should find him," Alexander told me, his voice rich with meaning.

I couldn't decide if he was being cautious due to the presence of the housekeeper, or because he wanted to wait for Smith to be here before he delivered bad news. I told myself it was the latter. After all, we'd gone out of our way to keep Mrs. Winters in the dark while knowing exactly where she was at all times. Alexander knew better than to share secrets in front of strangers. I imagined he'd spent his whole life learning to prevent the staff from overhearing the wrong thing.

I nodded and started toward the hall. Smith must have gone upstairs. He probably needed a moment away from our growing number of guests. I'd only gotten as far as the doorway when Georgia called, "Stop."

"What?" I asked, even though my body halted in place.

"You won't find him upstairs," she confessed.

A drum pounded in my head as I stared at her, trying to translate her words into any meaning other than the one I already knew to be true. "Where is he?"

"I can't tell you that."

"Georgia," I said, my voice low but filled with a dangerous undercurrent. "*Where* is he?"

"I heard you the first time," she said. "*I can't tell you.*"

"Then tell me," Alexander ordered, stepping to my side.

Georgia shook her head.

My knees locked, my legs feeling weak beneath me, and I nearly crumbled. It was only Penny, still nestled in my arms, that forced me to stay upright. Something was happening. Georgia knew where he had gone. Judging from the pinched look on her face, she didn't agree with whatever decision he had made.

Had he gone to take the fall for what I'd done? Was he on his way to the police to tell them he was responsible for Nora's disappearance?

"I don't think you understand," Alexander continued. "I need to talk to him."

"It might be too late for that," she admitted.

I took one shaky step toward the nearest chair. Edward shot out of his own seat, just in time to rescue Penny from my arms as I finally buckled. I didn't know what Georgia meant. I didn't understand her words. Somehow, my heart did, though, because I felt it break.

"Where is he?" Alexander's command boomed through the room, echoing in the vacant space my heart had recently occupied.

"Doing something stupid," Georgia said through gritted teeth. Her jaw tensed, and I could see the war going on inside her. At last, she exhaled with a frustrated grunt. "He got a blackmail letter today. You didn't kill anyone."

That statement was directed at me. Everything hurt too much. I couldn't process this, so I shook my head. "I don't understand."

"It's a game," she told me. "She always loved to play games."

"Who?" I asked, but before she could answer, Mrs. Winters appeared with a cake. She'd taken the time to ice the chocolate cake with delicate flowers and there was a single, oversized candle burning brightly at its center.

"Shall we sing?" she asked, sounding more cheery than

usual. She placed the cake on the table in the corner of the room, and continued, "Of course, we'll want to serve it in the dining room, but I thought..." She trailed off when she finally lifted her head to find us staring morosely at each other. "Is this a party or a funeral?"

I choked back a sob, and Edward sank into the chair next to me. He kept one arm around Penny, holding her carefully, and wrapped the other around my shoulder to pull me close.

"You brought a cake?" Alexander said out of nowhere. "But if you're..."

"Will someone explain what's going on?" Mrs. Winters said, looking put out. "I spent all day in the kitchen on that. You should sing a song and blow out your candle." When none of us moved, she turned and huffed back to the kitchen.

"Who is it?" I turned pleading eyes on Georgia. She opened her mouth to answer when I realized it didn't matter. Time was running out. There was only one thing to do now. I forced myself onto my feet. "Tell me where he is."

The time for requests was over. It didn't matter who my husband was facing, so much as that he was doing it without me. I had no idea what had driven Smith to such extreme measures, but I wasn't going to wait here while he did it.

"The pond," Georgia said in a strained voice as if she'd barely convinced herself to come clean.

"Stay with Penny," I told Edward before starting toward the kitchen.

"Where are you going?" he called.

"To find my husband." I barely made it two steps before Georgia's hand tightened over my arm and yanked me back.

"Let me go."

"I promised him," she hissed.

"I promised him!" I exploded. "And he promised me, and he is not going to face whatever this is alone."

"Of course he isn't," Alexander interjected. He turned and held out a hand to Brex. His guard studied him for a split second and, finally, sighed. Brex reached under his jacket and drew out a black handgun. He deposited it in the king's palm before drawing another from the other side.

I started toward the door again, and Georgia pulled me back one more time as a chorus of *no's* erupted from everyone.

"You can't ask me to stay here while he's in trouble!"

"No," Georgia agreed, "but I can ask you to stay here for your daughter."

Her words ripped through me, and I looked over to where Edward still held Penny, his own face masked in shock. She was right. I knew why Smith had left tonight. He'd done it to protect us—to protect his family. Whatever —whoever—was waiting for him had planned this.

"They want me to come, too." The realization slipped from my lips. If someone had wanted to hurt Smith or I they would have had plenty of chances to do so—individually. This was about something bigger than that. Someone wanted to hurt us. Someone wanted to break us. As strong as we were together, tonight we might be stronger apart.

"We'll handle this," Alexander promised, but Georgia stepped in front of him.

"*We'll* handle this. We're the bodyguards, remember?"

"She's got a point, Poor Boy," Brex agreed. "Someone needs to stay here. This might all be a ploy to get them alone." He hitched a thumb in my direction.

Alexander looked on the verge of detonation, but almost instantly he smirked. "Good point. We need security here. There are multiple potential targets. Brex, you need to stay behind."

"That is not—"

"Georgia, you will accompany me as my personal security. It's a better use of our resources. And I owe Smith Price, so don't make me put either of you down." The tone of his voice left no room for disagreement. At another time I might have marveled at his cunning manipulation of the situation, but now all I could think of was the ticking clock. He crossed closer to Brex and whispered something to him. Brex pulled back with surprise, but didn't say anything.

"We'd better get going." Georgia drew her own gun and looked to the clock on the mantle. "The letter told him to meet her at seven."

They started toward the door, but Alexander stopped and turned to his brother. "Edward..."

Their eyes met for just a moment, something unspoken passing between them. Edward rose from the leather wingback and cautiously handed me the baby. I held Penny like a life preserver, reminding myself that she was the reason I needed to let them take care of this. Then he turned and walked to his brother.

"If..." Alexander said.

The only thing any of us knew was that we had no idea what to expect. We'd seen too much to assume this would end happily.

"I know," Edward said when his brother couldn't finish. He clapped one hand on his brother's shoulder. "I've got her."

Alexander's throat slid, a tight smile flashing over his face, before he turned and nodded for Georgia to follow him. I didn't have to ask what he had meant. The message had been clear. Alexander knew that he was walking into the unknown, and he did so willingly. He also knew the risk that came with that. If he didn't return, Edward would be there for Clara. There was never really a question of that. But hearing him say it was what Alexander needed to hear. Despite everything that had happened and the sins that might never be forgiven, they were brothers before all us.

We watched them disappear. I tried to tell myself they would all walk back through these doors tonight—that our nightmare was finally over—but I knew better than to think my life was that simple.

"What did Alexander tell you?" Edward's voice interrupted my thoughts. "When he whispered in your ear?"

I realized they had been talking about something while I thought about Edward and his brother.

"It doesn't make sense much, unless..." Brex paused as if puzzling it. His eyes moved toward the cake waiting on the table with its single red candle still lit. Wax had melted down its side and puddled on the frosting in a pool of crimson. "He told me to watch Mrs. Winters."

"Why?" I asked, confused enough to be distracted from what was happening on Thornham's dark grounds.

His eyes lifted and met mine. "Because she's the Thorne baby."

27

SMITH

It wasn't Margot. I blinked, checking to see if the night was playing tricks with my eyes, and when they refocused, I finally saw it. She had been there the whole time, under our noses. I'd been too preoccupied with Belle and the baby to really look at her.

If I had, maybe I would have seen the truth. It was so obvious now. In a lot of ways they looked nothing alike—except for the dark hair. A wicked smile carved its way across her lips as I stared, a smile I'd never seen on her face before. A smile I had seen Margot wear so many times.

But it wasn't Margot.

"Nora," I said her name in confusion. There was a split second of relief. She was alive. Belle had nothing to do with her disappearance. Margot hadn't framed my wife for murder, like I'd believed all afternoon. But she wasn't the naive nanny she'd played. She wasn't a stranger that we'd welcomed into our home. I'd known her all along. I shook my head and called her by her full name—her real name. "Or should I say Honora?"

"Miss me?" she asked, wrinkling her nose. She sashayed across the frosty grass, looking nothing like the woman I'd trusted to care for my daughter. That didn't mean she was a stranger, though. There were remnants of the girl I'd known years ago, but Honora Pleasant had been a shy child, ten years her sister's junior, and as awkward as Margot was graceful. "I lost a little weight, got a little taller. I'm older, obviously. I don't know why I was worried that you would figure it out. Then again, I'd always been told you were smart."

I shook my head as a swarm of little moments invaded my brain. The picture of Margot in my desk that had appeared after she came to work for us. Nora had asked if she was my sister. She'd practically handed me the information. My fingers fumbled for the mobile phone in my pocket but I didn't dare take it out.

"You're seeing it more now, aren't you?" She laughed and the sound bounced around the night. "I *was* a little offended. But then, you never gave two shits about me. You only had eyes for her. Just like you only have eyes for Belle now."

"Belle is my wife," I growled.

"So was Margot. But you forgot her, too." She swirled her finger in the air before pausing it to point at me in accusation. "Everyone was expendable to you. Margot. Hammond. I'm surprised you showed up at all tonight. It was my final test."

"Test of what?" I pretended to be interested—part of

me was—while trying to get my bearings. I listened closely for other movements, something to indicate that she wasn't alone but the night was still.

"Love," she sang the word. "I kept waiting for you to betray Belle. How could you resist a hot nanny? Even her business partner said so. I overheard it when we went to lunch. "She reached to pluck a single leaf from a nearly naked tree branch. "And then when Belle was acting so strangely, when she put your precious daughter at risk, I thought that would be the end of it. But you stood by her. You never cared as much for Margot. You passed her around. Let other men fuck her. Let Hammond manipulate her."

"*She* let him do that," I corrected her. "Margot never did anything she didn't want to do." Somehow Nora had reimagined her sister as a fucking saint, but the truth was Margot was as twisted as all of us. She'd always burned a little brighter, though. She'd flown a little higher. Just like Icarus.

"That's what you think?" Nora snapped, her face contorting with feral rage. "Did you ever read her journals? Did you even bother to look through the things you sent to our mother after she died? It was just a box with an unsigned note..."

"I was young." But I knew it wasn't an excuse. After Margot's death, I'd been shaken to the core. Our marriage was nearly over before she'd been killed. We both knew it. Neither of us gave a fuck about making it work anymore. We were both more interested in money and what it could buy us. When she died, I closed the door to our bedroom and effectively shut her away. It was easier than asking myself if I was responsible for what had happened to her.

It was easier than admitting what I'd already known. I was.

"She was leaving you. She called to tell mother, but she got me instead. I was too young to understand and she was crying so hard. All I could make out was one thing. She told me, 'Nora, never let love break you.'"

"Margot didn't love me," I said in a sure voice. Everything I'd learned since her death pointed to that fact. I'd discovered her connection with the man who had warped my life into a nightmare. She had been planted in my life like a weed. I was lucky she hadn't taken me down along with her. "We were just kids, playing a game."

"Margot did love to play games." Nora nodded. "I read her journals. I know that. She began a game with you. Hammond asked her to. But she lost."

"She died," I corrected her. I wasn't certain there was a point. Nora was insane. I wasn't going to reach her. I wasn't going to change her mind.

"She lost!" Nora screamed and there was a flutter overhead as some dark, winged creature flew into the night. "Because she forfeited the game. She fell in love with you. She had everything she could want and so much more waiting for her. Hammond told her she had to stay, but you kept breaking her heart. She couldn't do it anymore."

"She didn't love me," I repeated feebly.

"No, Smith, *you* didn't love *her*," Nora said.

I knew she was right. I just couldn't admit it.

"I would never have hurt her." I was responsible for

marrying a woman I didn't love, but I'd stood by her. We'd taken lovers with each other's approval. We'd made a perverted version of a marriage work. Our arrangement seemed fine. I'd never really understood why it all fell apart—why she left that night.

Until now.

"So, I decided to return the favor—for my sister, you see," she continued. "Hammond kept a close eye on me all those years. I didn't have a big sister to do that anymore. I didn't have someone to protect me. My mother was never the same after Margot died. You never even bothered to check on either of us. Hammond had to do that. He took care of us. "

My stomach roiled, understanding too well what she meant. After my father's death, Hammond had groomed me—just as he had the rest of my family. It was Hammond's gift. He could find the darkness hidden in anyone and dig it out like a pig trained to root out truffles. Where others saw sad stories, he saw potential. Because sadness could be twisted, especially if you dangled poison that looked like love.

"I'm sorry that he hurt you," I said in a low voice.

"You hurt me," she spat back. "When you took my sister and used her. When you broke her heart. When you barely acknowledged that she died. Because once she was gone, Hammond showed me how the world worked."

I knew that lesson all too well.

"Imagine my surprise when Hammond told me you'd fallen for the woman he sent you—the woman you were meant to use just like Margot was meant to manipulate you. But you fell for her. I'd read Margot's journals, so I didn't believe it. You weren't capable of love. She knew it. She was sure of it. I drove to London from university and followed you both. And he was right! You did love this replacement. You didn't even remember Margot or how much she loved you."

"I moved on. That's the benefit of being the one left alive." It was a lesson she needed to learn next.

"For a while, I thought Hammond was going to deal with you—and then he didn't. That was a disappointment. I wish I knew who killed him, I would send them a thank you card. He was useless in the end."

"And you were free," I reminded her. "You could be free now. Go back to school. Move on with your life, like Margot would have wanted."

"Like she would have wanted?" Nora shook her head, sending her dark hair rippling over her shoulders. "She only wanted one thing: for you to pay. She wrote about it over and over again. She wanted you to hurt like she did. She wanted you to know what it was like to live without love." She paused for a moment and looked at me with round eyes, sparkling like the frost on the ground beneath us. "I didn't get to know my sister. Not well enough. Not until I read those journals. When I did, I knew what I had to do. I had to take the love you'd found away from you. Just like you did to my sister. Until you had nothing left. Just like my sister."

"So, I waited," she continued. "I watched you get married and run around with your privileged friends, all while ignoring the lives you destroyed. And then Belle got pregnant and you got cold feet about those friends of yours. You started looking for a house. I needed to get you in place. I knew it would be easier that way, so I tipped off the estate agency about Thornham. It passed to a trust after the old owners died. They couldn't list the property—not with its reputation around town. And not many people want to live like this anymore. But I knew you. Your bird needed a gilded cage. Then, once you were where I wanted you, I moved heaven and hell to get that interview with the agency. I read everything I could about Belle and her fashion empire. No one else was going to get that job. I wouldn't let them."

"How did you even know about Thornham?" I couldn't understand how everything led back to Nora. She was crazy—that much was clear. But she didn't have Hammond's resources or information network.

"A year after my sister died, I was committed to Brighton Sanatorium—"

Everything clicked into place. She'd been able to move heaven and hell as she said, because she'd already faced hell once.

"Everyone knew that story there. It was the warning cry. Get better or you'll wind up like her, stuck in your room, talking to the walls. She got out one day and screamed about Thornham and ghosts, and I never forgot that. She made it sound like the mouth of madness. When you decided to move to the country, I looked it up. I knew it was just the place for you, Smith," Nora grinned wickedly.

"You couldn't have known we would come here."

"Hammond told me once that there's two parts to

laying a trap," Nora said. "First, you come up with the snare. Thornham was my snare. It was everything you were looking for, but you kept going back to fucking London. So I had to figure out how to do the second thing he told me. He said you could wait forever for your prey to cross your trap, or you could send them running in its direction. I remembered that Margot wrote about the bullet you carried with you. The one you were saving to kill your father's murderer. So I sent you both a little present for the new baby."

"You sent the bullet?" How much time had we wasted searching for connections to MI-18? I should have seen the bullet as the clue it was: this had always been about me—about my past.

"I needed you to leave London. I needed you to call me to come help with the baby."

"And Belle needed you, but you betrayed her." I needed something to fight back with.

"Oh, she did most of the work herself at first," Nora said. "Credit where credit is due. She was so emotional and useless. It was pathetic, but you both just lapped up whatever help you could get. When she started acting crazy, you believed she was."

"I never—"

"You don't have to lie to me. You thought she was crazy. She thought she was crazy, too. That was easy enough to arrange, especially once I moved in. Antipsychotics can do funny things to people who aren't actually crazy. It's funny really."

"You gave her..." We'd trusted this woman. We'd let her

into our home, and she'd breached that trust. But not simply by lying. She had wormed her way into our worlds, depositing her wickedness every place she could find.

"It was simple. Wrong drugs. Wrong tea. I took the nappies she packed out of the bag, and she nearly melted. I whispered to her in her sleep. God, you sleep like a rock. I was so nervous the first time. I was sure I would wake you, Smith, but you didn't budge." She laughed with delight at the memory. "I didn't have to do much to twist the knife. Although personally, if I had to choose a favorite trick, it was the nuts. I know you're probably thinking: how could I top faking my own death? I mean, it *did* take effort to get all that mud on her, but she was so out of it after she took that pill. And it wasn't exactly easy to gather so much blood. But no, it has to be the nuts."

"You faked that, too?" I needed to keep her raving. I wanted her to spill every detail. I wanted to know everything.

"No." She giggled, turning in a circle. "I am allergic. It was a real risk. I think that's why it was so exciting. I made sure that my file was gone. I never put it on there, by the way. I never told Belle. I hid my Epi-Pen. I really could have died!"

"Thrilling," I bit out, wishing she had. Then the nightmare would have ended.

"Don't be a sore loser, Smith."

"Mr. Price," I growled.

"But we're family, remember?"

"What do you want from me?" I'd grown tired of her game. I could see every move now. And she was wrong about one thing: Nora thought she had me. She thought she could take me off the board or force me to choose between myself or my wife. She was wrong.

"To pay for your sins," she said. Her hands slipped out of her pocket. Moonlight caught the edge of a knife. She raised it over her head, her eyes wild, and I saw her final move. She would win the twisted game she thought we were playing, even at the cost of her life.

"No!" I moved toward her as a gunshot cracked through the air. I felt something whizz past my ear, and then Nora's body was flung into the air like a rag doll, her arms splayed and her eyes frozen in surprise. She hit the ground with a thump.

"Good shot." Alexander's voice floated through the fog. I turned to see him and Georgia appearing through the haze like ghosts walking through a wall. Both had guns still drawn.

I exhaled heavily and pulled my mobile out of my pocket. "I recorded her confession," I explained. Nora didn't need to die. Before this, I would have killed any person who hurt my family without blinking. But now, I saw things differently. How many lives had Hammond destroyed? I was wrong. It wasn't my sins that kept finding me. It was his. "She needed to be locked up. She needed to pay for what she'd done."

"Are you complaining about our—"

A scream split the air and I felt a blade pierce my shoulder. I stumbled forward, ducking just in time to give Alexander a clear shot. He took it without hesitation.

"You were saying?" he asked coolly.

I reached behind me and touched my shoulder. Drawing my hand back, I found it coated with blood.

"Let's get you back to your family," Georgia said softly, "and call a doctor."

"And maybe the police," Alexander suggested, leaning over to check Nora's body.

"That depends." Georgia raised an eyebrow, meeting my eyes. "Don't best friends bury the bodies?"

"Not this time," I told her. I wasn't going to hide from my past anymore. I wasn't going to let it define me. Instead, I left it behind in the dirt and walked away.

I stepped inside the back door and made my way toward the living room toward the fire and my daughter and my wife. Mrs. Winters flapped over, clucking at me. "Is this mud? My floors!"

I glanced back to see a trail of blood and dirt in my wake. "It's blood. I'm sorry my wound is making a mess."

Her neck snapped back and she turned to stare, not moving when Alexander and Georgia walked around her. I would deal with it later. I had to, unless I wanted to find another housekeeper. I wasn't sure her poor heart could take any more excitement between having the King of England for dinner and the shootout on the grounds.

Clutching my hand over the wound to staunch the bleeding, I walked wearily into the sitting room. Edward jumped up when he saw me, and Brex immediately headed to Alexander, ready for a report on what had transpired. But Belle lingered near the fireplace.

Penny's downy hair was visible just over her shoulder, glinting gold in the firelight. Belle moved rhythmically, rocking her, but the baby didn't make a sound. I realized she was doing it for herself as much as for Penny.

"Beautiful," I said softly, and her shoulders sagged as whatever weight she'd been holding on them released. She turned to me slowly. When our eyes met, a ragged sob escaped her lips.

Despite the exhaustion I felt, I walked swiftly toward her, forgetting my wound, forgetting everything but her. Belle rushed to meet me and we collided, her arms cradling Penny protectively as she pressed into my arms. Her free hand reached around to hook my neck, hitting the stab wound, and I winced. Her eyes widened and she started to draw back, but I was too quick.

I kissed her, knowing she was mine and that nothing could come between us. We had faced darkness behind these walls, not just from our enemy but from ourselves, and we were still here. We were still forever. Her mouth parted in a soft sigh, welcoming me home.

A throat cleared loudly and we broke apart.

"Sorry to interrupt, but I didn't save your ass so you could bleed to death from a stab wound," Alexander called from the door.

"You were stabbed?" Belle yelped in panic, waking Penny.

"Everyone relax. I'm putting pressure on it, the blood loss is already slowing." I leaned in to kiss the baby's head, smiling. I would never take simple acts like that for granted again.

We laid Penny down into the nursery and Georgia insisted on performing a security sweep. We returned to the sitting room to sort through the evening. We filled Belle in as Georgia inspected my wound, which turned out to only need cleaning and bandaging. Alexander and Brexton had called someone to help deal with the body. I wasn't surprised when a half-dozen black SUVs pulled onto the drive instead of the local police.

"I figured we'd skip the bumbling detective," he said. He took a deep breath and nodded. "Everything should be fine, but call me if there are any…issues. You have my number."

"Heading out?" I asked.

Alexander's eyes swept over us, and I knew what he was seeing: a family. "I think I'm ready to go home."

"Good, because Clara has been calling you nonstop," Brex said, pushing his mobile into his hands. "And I do not want to get blamed for keeping you out too late."

"This one is all on me."

Belle went to show them to the door. To my surprise, Edward went with her. I watched as the brothers said an awkward goodbye. At least they were talking to each other again. Before they could step out, Georgia flew into the entry, "Brex. A word."

He shared a quick look with Alexander, who tipped his head. "I'll prepare for the flight home. See you out there." He turned and met my eyes. "Remember, Price, you can call me anytime you get into trouble. Buckingham does get a little monotonous."

"Oh no," Belle interjected. "We are *all* going to have quiet, simple lives from now on."

Alexander bit back a bemused smile. "I'll try."

But as he stepped outside, his laughter echoed across the lawn. At least, he was developing a sense of humor about our fucked up lives.

A few minutes later, Brex marched across the foyer. His mouth was tightly drawn, and he forced a nod to both of us. "Good night."

"Night," we called after them.

Belle closed the door and sighed. "Will those two ever—"

"No," Georgia interrupted, coming into the room through the same door Brex had just used. "Which is exactly what I told him. I'm going to go wash all the psychopath off me. Try not to let anyone crazy in your house while I'm gone."

"That reminds me," Belle said, her eyes darting between us. "Mrs. Winters is—"

"Mrs. Winters is what?" The housekeeper appeared as if she'd been summoned.

Belle froze and studied her for a moment. Finally, she squared her shoulders and asked, "Are you adopted?"

"What?" Mrs. Winters placed a hand over her heart.

"I'm sorry," Belle added quickly. "I didn't mean to offend you."

"You...didn't," she said. "I don't know why it matters, but yes. I never knew a family other than the Winters. I was only a baby when I went to them."

My mouth hung open, but Georgia recovered quickly.

"Wait, you were adopted by the Winters, and you married a Winters?" she asked.

Mrs. Winters heaved a sigh, as though she was dealing with a lot of unruly children. "Housekeepers always go by missus—even the unmarried ones like me. Now, if you'll excuse me, I have a mess to clean up." She paused for a moment before looking at me. "I am glad you are okay, Mr. Price, and that the family is safe."

"Thank you," I murmured, meaning it.

"Do we tell her?" Belle asked after she'd left.

"Yes," I said before adding, "later."

"But what are we going to do now?"

I raised my hand to her lips and kissed it. "I have a few ideas."

"That's my cue," Georgia said.

I ignored her as I led my wife upstairs. My eyes never left her as we circled the spiral stairs. I knew each one would be there. I didn't need to look for them. I had complete faith. She'd given that to me. I might not have been a perfect man when Belle walked into my office and changed my life—maybe not even a good man. But she'd shown me to a path I thought I couldn't walk. Now I would choose no other.

This time when I moved between her legs and claimed her no shadows lingered over us. We had fought for each other. We had found each other. We always would. Belle's body pressed against mine, writing our future in pants and moans, as we sealed our vows to each other one more time.

When we finally collapsed, Belle laughed. It rang

through the room, sounding a new day had arrived at last. "I shouldn't be happy, right?"

I understood how she felt. We had only just escaped the darkness. There were still problems to deal with and wrongs that needed to be fixed. "I demand that you feel happy—now and every other day for the rest of your life."

"Is that so, Price?"

"It's an order."

"You've been spending too much time with the monarchy." But she burrowed closer to me under the sheets. She grew quiet for a moment. "Should we tell Mrs. Winters? That she's..."

"Yes." I didn't even have to consider it. "You can only be free of the past when you let it go. She deserves to know."

"But Thornham should be hers," Belle said softly.

I'd already considered that, too.

"Beautiful, let's go home," I murmured, my arms wrapped around her nude torso as my hand shamelessly covered her breast. After the last few months, she couldn't blame me for feeling possessive of her.

"Home?" she repeated, nuzzling against my chest. "I'm already home as long as I'm with you."

"London."

"London?" Her head raised to meet my eyes, surprise written across her face. It dimmed for a moment. She bit her lip. "For the weekend?"

I looked at her and knew that no matter what we faced, we would do it together. But that didn't mean we had to do it alone. We were stronger not only because of our love but because of the people who loved us. It might be dangerous and chaotic, but as long as I had her, I knew I had everything I needed. I couldn't escape my past. I had to embrace the future she'd given me. So there was no doubt when I answered her question that we belonged there.

"Forever."

ABOUT THE AUTHOR

GENEVA LEE is the *New York Times*, *USA Today*, and internationally bestselling author of over a dozen novels, including the Royals Saga which has sold two million copies worldwide. She lives in Washington state with her husband and three children, and she co-owns Away With Words Bookshop with her sister.

Geneva is married to her high school sweetheart. He's always the first person to read her books. Sometimes, he reads as she writes them. Last year, they were surprised by finding out Geneva was pregnant with their third child. They welcomed a beautiful baby girl in 2020.

When she isn't working or writing, Geneva likes to read, bake ridiculous cakes, and watch television. She loves to travel and is always anxious to go on a new adventure.

Printed in Great Britain
by Amazon